Maigret
and the Nahour Case

Georges Simenon

❧❧❧

MAIGRET
and the
Nahour Case

Translated by
Alastair Hamilton

A Helen and Kurt Wolff Book

A Harvest/HBJ Book
Harcourt Brace Jovanovich, Publishers
San Diego   New York   London

Requests for permission to make copies
of any part of the work should be mailed to:
Permissions, Harcourt Brace Jovanovich, Publishers,
Orlando, Florida 32887.

Library of Congress Cataloging in Publication Data
Simenon, Georges, 1903–
Maigret and the Nahour case.
Translation of: Maigret et l'affaire Nahour.
I. Title.
PQ2637.I53M25713   1982   843′.912   82-47661
ISBN 0-15-155559-1   AACR2
ISBN 0-15-655149-7 (Harvest/HBJ : pbk.)

Printed in the United States of America
First American edition 1982
First Harvest/HBJ edition 1986
A B C D E F G H I J K

Maigret
and the Nahour Case

HE HAD BEEN SEIZED BY THE SHOULDER AND WAS STRUGgling. He even tried to throw a punch, with the humiliating feeling that his arm would not do what he wanted, but lay inert and stiff.

"Who is it?" he shouted, vaguely realizing the inadequacy of the question.

Did he really make a sound?

"Jules! . . . Telephone . . ."

He had heard a menacing noise in his sleep, but he had not thought for a minute that it was the telephone ringing, that he was lying in bed, that he was having a nightmare, which he had already forgotten, and that his wife was shaking him.

He automatically put out his hand to pick up the receiver as he opened his eyes and sat up. Madam Maigret was also sitting up in the warm bed, and the bedside lamp next to her shed a soft, intimate light.

"Hello . . ."

He repeated what he had said in his dream:

"Who is it?"

"Maigret? . . . Pardon speaking . . ."

The Superintendent could just see the time on the alarm clock on his wife's night table. It was half past one. They had left the Pardons soon after eleven, after their monthly dinner, which had consisted of a tasty shoulder of mutton.

"Yes . . . I'm listening. . . ."

"I'm sorry to wake you up so early. . . . Something has just happened here that seems quite serious to me: it's up your street. . . ."

The Maigrets and the Pardons had been friends and had dined together once a month for almost ten years, and yet it had never occurred to the two men to be on Christian-name terms.

"I'm listening, Pardon. . . . Go on. . . ."

The voice at the other end of the line sounded anxious, embarrassed.

"I think it would be better if you came to see me. . . . You'd understand the situation better."

"I hope there hasn't been an accident."

A pause.

"No . . . Not exactly, but I'm worried. . . ."

"Is your wife all right?"

"Yes. She's making us some coffee."

Madame Maigret was trying to figure out what was going on from her husband's answers, and she looked at him questioningly.

"I'll be there at once."

He hung up. Wide awake by now, he looked anxious. It was the first time that Doctor Pardon had called him like this, and the Superintendent knew him well enough to know that it must be serious.

4

"What's going on?"

"I don't know. . . . Pardon needs me."

"Why didn't he come and see you?"

"There seems to be a reason for me to go there."

"He was in a very good mood when we saw him. . . . So was his wife. We talked about his daughter and son-in-law, and the cruise they were going to make to the Balearic Islands next summer. . . ."

Was Maigret listening? He dressed uneasily, trying to figure out, in spite of himself, why the doctor had telephoned.

"I'll make you some coffee."

"No point . . . Madame Pardon is already making some."

"I'll call a taxi, shall I?"

"Either you won't find one in this weather, or else it'll take half an hour to get here. . . ."

It was January 14—Friday, January 14—and the temperature in Paris had been twelve degrees below zero all day. The snow, which had fallen abundantly in recent days, had frozen so hard that it was impossible to sweep it away, and, in spite of the salt strewn on the sidewalks, there were still some patches of sheer ice on which pedestrians would slip.

"Put on your heavy scarf . . ."

A thick woolen scarf which she had knitted for him and which he hardly ever had a chance to wear.

"Don't forget your galoshes . . . Can't I come with you?"

"Why should you?"

She didn't like seeing him go out alone that night. On their way back from the Pardons', as they were walking along cautiously, watching the sidewalk in front

5

of them, Maigret had fallen heavily at the corner of Rue du Chemin-Vert, and he had remained seated on the ground for some time, dazed and ashamed of himself.

"Did you hurt yourself?"

"No . . . I was just surprised."

He had not allowed her to help him up or to hold him by the arm.

"There's no point in our both falling. . . ."

She followed him to the door, kissed him, and murmured: "Be careful . . ."

Then she left the door ajar until he got to the ground floor. Maigret avoided Rue du Chemin-Vert, where he had fallen so recently; he preferred to make a slight detour along Boulevard Richard-Lenoir to Boulevard Voltaire, where the Pardons lived.

He walked slowly, not hearing any footsteps except his own. There was neither a taxi nor a car in sight. Paris seemed empty, and he could remember having seen it like that, congealed with cold, only two or three times in his life.

On Boulevard Voltaire, however, the throttled-back engine of a truck was running near Place de la République, and Maigret could see the dark silhouettes of men throwing shovelfuls of salt onto the sidewalk.

The light was on in two windows of the Pardons' apartment, the only lighted windows in the row of houses. Maigret could just make out a dark shadow behind the curtains, and when he got to the door, it opened before he had time to ring.

"I'm sorry, Maigret. . . ."

Pardon was wearing the same navy blue jacket he had worn at dinner.

"I'm in such a tricky situation that I really don't know what to do."

In the elevator the Superintendent noticed that his face looked strained.

"Haven't you been to bed?"

And the doctor started to explain awkwardly:

"I wasn't sleepy when you left, so I decided to fill in the files I was behind with."

In other words, in spite of his work, he had not wanted to postpone the traditional dinner.

Strangely enough, the Maigrets had stayed later than usual. The main topic of conversation had been vacations, and Pardon had observed that his patients were increasingly tired when they returned home, particularly after organized tours.

They went through the waiting room, where a single lamp was lit, but instead of going into the living room, they went into Pardon's office.

Madame Pardon arrived soon after with a tray, two cups, a coffeepot, and some sugar.

"Please forgive me for appearing like this. . . . I didn't bother to dress. . . . Anyhow, I won't stay a moment, because it's my husband who wants to speak to you."

She was wearing a pale-blue bathrobe over her night-gown, and her feet were bare in her slippers.

"He didn't want to bother you. . . . I insisted, and if I'm wrong I'm sorry. . . ."

She poured out the coffee and went to the door.

"Since I won't be asleep, you must call me if you need anything. . . . Are you hungry, Maigret?"

"I had too good a dinner to be hungry."

"How about you?"

"No thanks."

The door to the little room where the doctor examined his patients was open. In the middle of the room stood a high surgical table covered by a sheet stained with blood, and Maigret noticed some large patches of blood on the green linoleum.

"Sit down . . . Drink your coffee first . . ."

He pointed to a heap of papers and cards on the desk.

"You see . . . People don't realize that we have a bureaucrat's job to do besides consultations and visits. . . . Since we frequently get urgent calls, we put it off, and then, one fine day, we're submerged by it. . . . I thought I could spend two or three hours at it."

Pardon started his rounds at eight in the morning, before seeing patients in his office at ten o'clock. The Picpus quarter is not a rich one. It is full of poor people, and there were frequently up to fifteen patients in the waiting room. Few of the monthly dinners ended without a call that would keep Pardon out for an hour or more.

"I was engrossed in these papers. . . . My wife was asleep. . . . I didn't hear a sound until the front doorbell suddenly rang and made me jump. When I went to the door, I saw a couple on the landing who looked rather odd to me."

"Why?"

"First of all, because I knew neither the man nor the woman, and usually my patients are the only people who call on me in the middle of the night—or, rather, the ones who haven't got a telephone."

"I see."

"Then, I didn't think they lived in my district.

8

The woman was wearing a sealskin coat and hat. . . .
It so happened that my wife was looking through
a fashion magazine two days ago, and suddenly said
to me:

" 'If you ever get me a coat, don't give me a mink,
but a sealskin. . . . Mink has become so common, but
seal . . .'

"I didn't listen to anything else, but I remembered
that when I was standing at the door, looking at them
in amazement.

"The man was also wearing clothes one doesn't usually see on Boulevard Voltaire.

"He was the one who asked, with a slight foreign
accent:

" 'Doctor Pardon?'

" 'That's me, yes.'

" 'This lady had just been injured, and I wondered
whether you could see her.'

" 'How did you get my address?'

" 'An elderly lady walking down Boulevard Voltaire
gave it to us. . . . I suppose she's a patient of yours.'

"They came into my office. The woman was very
pale. She seemed about to faint and looked at me with
large, expressionless eyes, clutching her chest with both
her hands.

" 'I think you should hurry, Doctor,' said the man,
taking off his gloves.

" 'What sort of a wound is it?'

"He turned to the woman, who had very fair hair
and must have been under thirty.

" 'You'd better take off your coat. . . .'

"Without a word she took off her fur coat, and I saw

9

that the back of her straw-colored dress was soaked with blood down to the waist.

"Look, there's a bloodstain on the carpet, next to my desk, where she stood, unsteadily.

"I made her go into the surgery and offered to help her take off her dress. Without even saying a word, she shook her head and undressed by herself.

"The man didn't follow us, but the door between the two rooms was open and he continued to talk to me, or, rather, to answer me. I had put my white coat on and washed my hands. The woman lay motionless on her stomach, without a groan."

"What time was it?" asked Maigret, who had just lit his first pipe since the telephone call.

"I looked at the clock when the bell rang. It said ten past one. It all happened very quickly, far more quickly than it takes to tell you the story.

"In fact, I was already washing the wound and staunching the blood when I realized what had happened. At first sight, the wound was not too deep. It was in the back, on the right-hand side: a wound about six inches long, with the blood still flowing.

"As I worked I asked the man, who was out of sight in my office:

" 'Tell me what happened.'

" 'I was walking along Boulevard Voltaire, about a hundred yards from here, and this lady was in front of me. . . .'

" 'You're not going to say she slipped?'

" 'No . . . I was rather surprised to see her alone in the street at this time of night, and I walked slowly so that she wouldn't think I was trying to pick her up. . . . That was when I heard a car. . . .' "

10

Pardon stopped to drink his coffee and pour a second cup.

"Do you want some?"

"I'd love some."

Maigret was still sleepy, his eyelids were stinging, and he felt like he was getting a cold. Ten of his detectives were in bed with the flu, and that had complicated his work in the last few days.

"I'm repeating our conversation as accurately as possible but I can't swear to every word. . . . I discovered that the wound was deeper between the third and fourth ribs, and as I was disinfecting it something fell to the floor, without my immediately noticing it."

"A bullet?"

"Wait a minute . . . The man in the next room went on:

" 'When the car drew level with this lady, it slowed down, nearly to a standstill, and I saw an arm stretch out of the door . . .' "

Maigret interrupted:

"The front door or the back door?"

"He didn't say, and it didn't occur to me to ask him. . . . Don't forget that I was performing a surgical operation. . . . I occasionally have to do this, in emergencies, but it isn't something I specialize in and I found the whole business rather strange. What surprised me most was the silence of the patient.

"The man continued:

" 'I heard an explosion and I saw this lady stagger, try to catch hold of the wall of a house, and then bend her knees and slowly sink into the snow.

" 'The car had driven away and had turned right, into a street I didn't know.

11

" 'I rushed forward. . . . I saw that she wasn't dead, and she helped herself up by clinging on to me.

" 'I asked her if she was wounded, and she nodded.'

" 'She didn't talk to you?'

" 'No . . . I didn't know what to do. I looked around for help. . . . An old woman was passing, and I asked her where I could find a doctor. She pointed to your house and gave me your name.' "

Pardon stopped talking and looked at Maigret like a truant child. It was the Superintendent who asked:

"Didn't it occur to the man to take her to a hospital?"

"I said the same thing. I said we were very close to Pitié and not far from Saint-Antoine. He just muttered:

" 'I didn't know that.' "

"I suppose he didn't know that the local police station was a hundred yards away either?"

"I don't suppose so. . . . I was embarrassed. . . . I know I had no right to attend to a wound caused by a fire arm without alerting the police immediately. But on the other hand, I had already started. . . . I told them:

" 'I'm just giving first-aid treatment, and when I've finished I'll call an ambulance.'

"I put on a temporary dressing.

" 'Don't wear those bloodstained clothes: I'll give you a bathrobe.'

"She shook her head and a few minutes later she put on her clothes and joined the man in my office.

"I said to both of them:

" 'Sit down . . . I'll be with you in a minute.'

"I wanted to take off my rubber gloves, my stained coat, and close the bottles I'd been using. I went on talking:

12

" 'You must both give me your name and address. . . . If you prefer a private clinic to a hospital, say so, and I'll see to it.' "

Maigret had already understood.

"How long did you leave them alone?"

"I can't be sure. . . . I remember picking up the bullet, which had fallen while I was dressing the wound, and throwing away the bloodstained swabs and bandages. . . . Two or three minutes? . . . As I was talking I went to the door and saw that my office was empty.

"First I rushed into the hall, and then to the landing. . . . Not hearing either the elevator or steps on the stairs, I came back to my office and looked out the window, but I couldn't see the sidewalk by the building.

"It was then that I clearly heard a car drive off. . . . I could swear that it sounded like a powerful car, a sports model. . . . By the time I'd opened the window, Boulevard Voltaire was empty except for a salt truck near Place de la République and one solitary figure far off in the other direction."

Apart from his closest collaborators—Lucas, Janvier, Torrence, and, more recently, young Lapointe, of whom Maigret was very fond—Doctor Pardon was the Superintendent's only friend.

There was just a year's difference in their ages, and each day both men inspected the diseases of men and society, so that their attitude was fairly similar.

They could chat for hours after their monthly dinners on Boulevard Richard-Lenoir and Boulevard Voltaire without noticing the time, and the experiences they described were almost identical.

Was it the mutual respect they felt that stopped them from calling each other by their Christian names?

13

On this night, in the tranquillity and silence of the doctor's office, they were not as relaxed as they had been a few hours earlier, maybe because they were facing each other on a professional level for the first time in their lives.

Intimidated, the doctor was talking faster than usual and he was obviously in a hurry to prove his good faith, just as though he were being interrogated by the Public Prosecutor. On his side, Maigret restrained himself from asking too many questions, asking those he considered indispensable only after a moment's hesitation.

"Look, Pardon, at the beginning you said that neither the man nor the woman seemed to be from this district."

The doctor tried to explain.

"Most of my patients are shopkeepers, workmen, and poor people. I'm not a society doctor, or a specialist, but a doctor who lugs his case up five or six floors twenty times a day. There are some well-to-do, middle-class apartment houses on this street, but I've never seen people who look anything like the couple I've just seen.

"Although the woman didn't say a word, I have a feeling she's a foreigner. . . . She looks very Nordic, with a milky complexion, fair hair, which one rarely sees in Paris unless it's dyed, and hers wasn't. . . . Judging from her breasts, I'd say that she'd had one or more children and that she'd nursed them. . . ."

"Any special peculiarities?"

"No . . . Just a minute . . . A scar about an inch long running from the left eye toward the ear . . . I noticed that because it looked like a wrinkle, which is quite attractive on a very young face."

14

"Do you think she remained silent voluntarily?"

"I'd swear to it. . . . Just as I would have sworn, when I saw them on the landing, and then in my office, that they knew each other intimately. . . . I may be wrong. But I believe that there's a sort of aura around couples who are deeply in love, and that even when they aren't looking at each other, when they aren't touching each other, one can feel a tie between them."

"Tell me about him."

"I saw less of him than of her, and he never took off his coat, made of a soft, supple material."

"Did he have a hat?"

"No. He was bareheaded. Brown hair, fine features, a sunburned skin, dark eyes. I'd say he was twenty-five or -six, and judging from his voice, his movements, and his clothes, I would say that he'd been brought up with a certain amount of money. A handsome boy, gentle-looking, rather melancholy . . . Probably Spanish or South American . . .

"What shall I do now? Since I don't know their names, I can't fill in their medical card. . . . Well, it's probably a case of criminal assault."

"Did you believe the man's story?"

"I didn't really think at the time. . . . It was only when I saw that my office was empty, and while I waited for you after my telephone call, that his account seemed rather strange."

Maigret examined the bullet attentively.

"Probably shot from a 6.35 . . . A weapon that's really dangerous only at point-blank range and is usually inaccurate."

"That would account for the wound. The bullet had

struck her back at an angle, grazing over several inches of skin before lodging between two ribs."

"How far can the woman go?"

"I can't tell. She may well have taken a sedative before coming, because she didn't react, and superficial wounds are often the most painful."

"Look, Pardon," muttered Maigret, getting up, "I'll see to them. Send me a statement tomorrow morning, repeating what you've just told me."

"Will I be in any trouble?"

"You're obliged to help somebody in danger, aren't you?"

He lit another pipe before putting on his hat and gloves.

"I'll keep in touch."

Outside, the air was icy, and gazing at the snow heaped against the buildings, he walked a hundred yards without seeing any bloodstains or signs of a fall. Then, retracing his steps, he crossed Place Léon Blum and went into the police station on the ground floor of one of the municipal buildings.

He had known Sergeant Demarie, sitting behind the counter, for years.

"Hello, Demarie."

Surprised to see the chief of the Crime Squad appear like that, Demarie looked rather embarrassed, because he had been reading a comic.

"Hello, Louvelle."

Constable Louvelle was making coffee on a kerosene stove.

"Did either of you hear anything an hour or so ago?"

"No, sir."

"Anything like a shot about a hundred yards away?"

"Nothing."

"Between one and ten past?"

"In what direction?"

"Boulevard Voltaire, Place de la République end."

"A two-man patrol, Constables Mathis and Bernier, went out at eleven o'clock exactly, down Boulevard Voltaire to Rue Amelot."

"Where are they now?"

The Sergeant glanced at the electric clock.

"Near the Bastille, unless they've got to Rue de la Roquette . . . They'll both be back at three. . . . Shall I try to get hold of them?"

"No . . . Get me a taxi . . . and call me at the Police Judiciare when they get here."

It took two or three calls before they could find a free taxi. Maigret telephoned his apartment.

"Don't worry if I'm not back till dawn. . . . I'm at the local police station. . . . A cab's coming for me. . . . No, no! . . . He's got nothing to do with what's just happened. . . . But I've got to see to it right now. . . . No, I didn't fall. . . . See you later. . . ."

The taxi passed the salt truck, which was driving at walking pace, and they came across only three cars before reaching Quai des Orfèvres, where the sentry at the gate looked stiff with cold.

Upstairs, he found Lucas, with Inspectors Jussieu and Lourtie. The rest of the premises appeared to be empty.

"Good evening, boys . . . To start with, call all the hospitals and private clinics in Paris. I want to know whether two people, a man and a woman, appeared after half past one. It's possible that the woman, who

17

is wounded in the back, turned up on her own. . . . Here's the description."

He tried to repeat Pardon's words.

"Start with the eastern districts."

While the three men rushed to the telephones, he went into his office, turned on the light, and took off his overcoat and his heavy knitted scarf.

He didn't believe the story about the shot from the car in the street. Those were gangster tactics, and he'd never seen a gangster with a 6.35. Besides, only one shot was fired, and that's rare in an attack from a car.

Like Pardon, he was sure that the man and the woman knew each other. Wasn't this proved by the fact that they left without a word, like accomplices, while the doctor was tidying up his surgery?

He went back to his three men, who had almost got to the end of their lists.

"Nothing?"

"No, chief."

He called the operator on the Emergency switchboard.

"Did you get any calls at about one in the morning? Did anyone report a shot?"

"Just a minute . . . I'll ask the others. . . ."

And, a few seconds later:

"Only a brawl and a knife thrust in a bistro at Porte d'Italie . . . Requests for ambulances on account of broken arms and legs . . . Now that nearly everybody's reached home they're less frequent, but we still get a call about every ten minutes. . . ."

He had hardly hung up when Lucas called him.

"Phone for you, chief."

It was Demarie, from the police station in the Twelfth Arrondissement.

"The patrol has just got back. . . . Mathis and Bernier didn't see anything irregular and have reported only a few falls on ice patches. But Mathis noticed a red Alfa Romeo parked in front of 76b Boulevard Voltaire, and he even said to his partner:

" 'That's what we need for our rounds.' "

"What time was it?"

"Between five and ten past one. Mathis automatically stroked the hood and noticed that it was still warm."

In other words, the man and the woman had just gone into the building where they'd rung at the doctor's door at ten past one.

How had they got Pardon's address? When he was asked, Mathis said that he hadn't noticed an old woman in the whole street.

Where had the couple come from? Why had they parked almost in front of the police station on Boulevard Voltaire?

It was too late to warn the radio cars, because the red car had had time to reach its destination, wherever that might be.

Maigret muttered something, knitting his brows and taking short puffs at his pipe, and Lucas tried to make out what he was saying.

". . . foreigners . . . Spanish-looking . . . the woman didn't say anything . . . because she can't speak French? . . . Nordic-looking . . But why Boulevard Voltaire and why Pardon?"

That was what vexed him most. If the couple lived in Paris, it was almost certainly in a chic district, and

there are doctors on nearly every street in town. . . .
If the shot had been fired in a building, why not call a
doctor instead of carting the wounded woman through
the streets at twelve degrees below zero?

What if they were passing through, staying in a big
hotel? . . . It was unlikely. The noise of a shot rarely
goes unnoticed. . . .

"Why are you looking at me like that?" he asked
Lucas brusquely, as though he had just realized he was
standing there.

"I'm waiting for you to tell me what to do."

"How should I know?"

He grinned at his own attitude.

"It's an unlikely tale, and I don't know where to
begin. Apart from the fact that I was awakened by the
telephone in the middle of some nightmare . . ."

"Would you like a cup of coffee?"

"I've just had one. . . . A Spanish-looking fellow and
a Nordic-looking woman rang at my friend Pardon's
door at ten past one this morning. . . ."

As he told the story, sulkily he began to realize the
weak points.

"The shot wasn't fired in a hotel. Or in the street. It
must have been in an apartment or a private house."

"Do you think they're married?"

"I don't think so, although I can't say why. If they'd
called their normal doctor, provided they've got one,
he would have had to report to the police. . . ."

What intrigued him most was why they chose Pardon,
an obscure district doctor. Did they pick his name out
of the directory, at random?

"The woman isn't in any hospital or clinic. . . . Pardon offered to lend her one of his wife's bathrobes because her clothes were soaked with blood. She chose to put them on again. . . . Why?"

Lucas opened his mouth, but the Superintendent had already found an answer.

"Because they intended to escape. . . . I don't claim that to be a brilliant conclusion, but it makes sense."

"Most of the roads are unfit for traffic. . . . Particularly with a wounded passenger in the car . . ."

" I'd thought of that, too. . . . Call Breuker at Orly . . . If he isn't there, get me his idiot assistant, whose name I can never remember."

Breuker, an Alsatian who had never got rid of his accent, was superintendent at the airport. He wasn't on duty, and it was his assistant who replied.

"Assistant Superintendent Marathieu speaking."

"This is Maigret," muttered the head of the Crime Squad, irritated by the pretentious voice at the other end of the line.

"What can I do for you, sir?"

"I don't know yet. . . . How many foreign departures have you had since two o'clock, or, rather, since two-thirty this morning?"

"Only two . . . One flight to Amsterdam and another to India, via Geneva . . . All departures have been suspended for the last forty minutes because of ice on the runways."

"Are you far from the parking lot?"

"Not very, but it's not easy to walk outside, again because of the ice."

"Would you be so kind as to see if a red Alfa Romeo is parked there?"

21

"Have you got the number?"

"No. There can't be many red Alfa Romeos in your lot at this time of night. . . . If you find it, ask the passport inspectors whether they have seen a couple answering to the following description . . ."

He repeated what he had told Lucas and the others.

"Call me as soon as possible at the Quai des Orfèvres."

And Maigret, shrugging his shoulders, added as he turned toward Lucas:

"One never knows."

It was an odd investigation, and one would have said that the Superintendent wasn't taking it very seriously, that he was doing it rather as one does a crossword puzzle.

"Marathieu must be livid," commented Lucas. "Imagine sending someone as fussy and conceited as he is splashing about in the snow and doing balancing tricks on the ice!"

It was about twenty minutes before the telephone rang again. Maigret said mockingly:

"Assistant Superintendent Marathieu speaking."

And they were the first words he heard.

"Well, the red car?"

"There is a red Alfa Romeo in the parking lot, with a Paris plate."

"Is it locked?"

"Yes . . . A couple answering to the description you gave me took the 3:10 flight to Amsterdam."

"Have you got their names?"

"The inspector who checked them can't remember the names. He can only remember the passports. The man had a Colombian passport and the woman a Dutch one. Both passports were full of visas and stamps."

"What time do they arrive in Amsterdam?"

"If there's no delay and the runway is fit for landing, they touch down at 4:17."

It was 4:22. The couple were probably showing their passports and going through customs. At any rate, at this stage in the investigation Maigret could hardly apply directly to the police at the Dutch airport.

"Well, chief? What shall I do?"

"Nothing. Wait to be relieved. As for me, I'm going to bed. Good night, boys . . . Incidentally, will one of you drive me home?"

Half an hour later he was sleeping soundly next to his wife.

❧ 2 ❧

SOME CASES APPEAR DRAMATIC FROM THE START AND GET right into the headlines of the newspapers. Others, which seem banal, get only three or four lines on the sixth page before one realizes that a mere news item was really concealing a drama shrouded in mystery.

Maigret was having his breakfast, sitting opposite his wife, near the window. It was half past eight in the morning, and it was so dark that all the lights had to be on. Since he hadn't slept enough, he felt heavy, his mind dull, full of confused ideas.

There was some frost in the corners of the window-panes, and he remembered that when he was a child he used to make drawings or write his initials in it; he also recalled the curious feeling, both painful and agree-able, when the thin film of frost got under his finger-nails.

After three very cold days it had started snowing again, and one could hardly see the houses and shops on the other side of the street.

"You're not too tired?"

"One more cup of coffee and I'll be in fine form."

In spite of himself he tried to imagine the couple of elegant foreigners who had suddenly appeared, God knows where from, in the local doctor's waiting room. Pardon had immediately sensed that they belonged to another world, different from his own, Maigret's, and the Picpus district in which they both lived.

The Superintendent had frequently had to deal with people like this, people as much at home in London as in New York or Rome, who take an airplane the way most people take the subway, stay in palaces in whatever country they go to, where they find their own friends, with similar habits, and form a sort of international freemasonry.

Not only a freemasonry of money, but also one of a certain sort of life, certain attitudes, even a certain set of morals, different from the morals of the ordinary human being.

Maigret never felt quite at ease with them, and he had difficulty in overcoming an irritation that could be mistaken for jealousy.

"What are you thinking about?"

"Nothing."

He wasn't aware of thinking. He was in a daze, and he started when he heard the telephone ring. It was now quarter to nine, and he was just going to get up from the table and put on his overcoat.

"Hello."

"Lucas here."

Lucas was due to go off duty at nine o'clock.

"I've just had a call from Superintendent Manicle of

25

the Fourteenth Arrondissement, chief. A man was killed last night in a small private house on Avenue du Parc-Montsouris. . . . A man named Nahour, a Lebanese. The cleaning woman found the body when she started work at eight o'clock."

"Has Lapointe arrived?"

"I think I hear him in the corridor. Just a minute . . . Yes . . . It's him all right."

"Tell him to come and fetch me by car. Tell Manicle that I'll be there as soon as I can. You can go to bed."

Maigret repeated under his breath:

"Nahour . . . Nahour . . ."

Another foreigner. The couple of the night before consisted of a Dutch woman and a Colombian. Now for Nahour and the Near East.

"A new case?" asked his wife.

"A crime, apparently, on Avenue du Parc-Montsouris."

He wrapped the large scarf around his neck, put on his coat, grabbed his hat.

"Aren't you going to wait for Lapointe?"

"I must get a breath of fresh air."

So Lapointe found him standing on the sidewalk. Maigret slipped into the little black car.

"Have you got the right address?"

"Yes, chief. It's the last house before the park, a house in the middle of a garden. . . . You can't have had much sleep last night."

The traffic was slow and tiresome. Here and there a car had skidded and stood immobilized in the middle of the road. On the sidewalks the pedestrians walked cautiously. The Seine was dark green, full of blocks of ice slowly drifting along the surface of the water. They stopped in front of a villa with part of the ground floor glassed in. The building must have been designed in 1925 or 1930, at a time when houses, then ultramodern, had sprung up in certain districts of Paris, particularly at Auteuil and Montparnasse.

A policeman on duty saluted the Superintendent and opened an iron gate leading into a small garden, in which stood a bare tree.

The two men walked along the path, climbed the four steps to the entrance, and found another policeman in the hall, who showed them into the study.

Manicle was there with one of his detectives. He was a small, thin man with a mustache, whom Maigret had known for over twenty years, and the two men shook hands. The District Superintendent then pointed to a body lying behind a mahogany desk.

"The cleaning woman, named Louise Bodin, informed us by telephone at five past eight. She starts work at eight every day. She lives nearby, on Rue du Saint-Gothard."

"Who is Nahour?"

"Felix Nahour was forty-two years old, a Lebanese citizen, with no known profession. He moved into this house six months ago, and he rents it furnished from a painter who has left for the United States."

It was very hot in the room in spite of the huge windows, partly covered with frost, as on Boulevard Richard-Lenoir.

"Were the curtains open when you arrived?"

"No. They were drawn. . . . As you see, they're thick curtains, padded with felt to stop the cold getting in."

"Has the doctor been here?"

"A local doctor came a moment ago and confirmed that he was dead, which is all too obvious. . . . I've informed the Medical Examiner, and he should be arriving at any minute, with the Public Prosecutor."

Maigret turned to Lapointe.

"Call Moers and tell him to come around at once with his men from the Records Office. . . . No, not from here. There may be some fingerprints on the receiver. You'll find a bistro or a phone booth nearby."

He took off his coat and his scarf, because, after an almost sleepless night, the heat was going to his head and making him dizzy.

The room was enormous. The floor was covered with pale blue moquette, and the furniture, although dissimilar, was in good taste and of considerable value.

As he went around the Empire desk to look at the dead man more closely, the Superintendent saw a photograph in a silver frame near the blotter.

It was the portrait of a young woman, with very fair hair and a sad smile, who had a little girl of around three next to her and a baby about a year old on her knees.

Knitting his brows, he seized the frame and, staring at the picture, he saw a scar about an inch long running from her left eye toward her ear.

"Is that his wife?"

"I suppose so. I've looked her up in our files. She is registered under the name of Evelina Nahour, maiden name Wiemars, born in Amsterdam."

"Is she in the house?"

"No. We knocked at her door. When there was no

answer, we opened it. The room is a bit untidy, but the bed has not been slept in."

Maigret bent over the crumpled body. He could see only half the face, but as far as he could judge without moving the man, a bullet had gone into his throat, severing the carotid and leaving a vast pool of blood on the carpet.

Nahour was fairly small, plump, and had a short brown mustache. He was going slightly bald. He wore a wedding ring on his left hand, which was carefully manicured, and he had tried to stop the blood flowing with his right hand.

"Do you know who was living in this house?"

"I've questioned the cleaning woman only briefly, thinking that you would rather do that. I then asked the secretary and the maid to stay upstairs, where one of my men is making sure they don't speak to one another."

"Where is this Madame Bodin?"

"In the kitchen . . . Shall I call her?"

"Please."

Lapointe had just come in, saying:

"I've done it, chief. . . . Moers is on his way."

Louise Bodin came in, with a defiant and obstinate expression. Maigret knew that type, the type of most Parisian cleaning women, women who have suffered, who have been ill-treated by life, and who hopelessly await an even more unpleasant old age. They harden, become suspicious, and consider the whole world responsible for their misfortunes.

"Your name is Louise Bodin?"

"Madame Bodin, yes."

29

She emphasized the *Madame,* which she regarded as her last remnant of feminine dignity. Her dark clothes hung on a thin body and her dark eyes were so intense that they looked almost feverish.

"Are you married?"

"I was."

"Is your husband dead?"

"If you really want to know, he's at Fresnes, and that's the best place for him."

Maigret preferred to not ask about the details of her husband's imprisonment.

"Have you been working here long?"

"Five months tomorrow."

"How did you get the job?"

"I answered an advertisement. . . . Before that I did an hour here, a morning or an afternoon there."

She laughed unpleasantly, turning to the corpse:

"It's interesting they put 'steady job' in the advertisement!"

"You don't sleep here?"

"Never. I went home at eight in the evening and I came back at eight the next morning."

"Didn't Monsieur Nahour have any profession?"

"He must have done something, since he had a secretary and used to spend hours deep in papers."

"Who is his secretary?"

"A fellow from his country, Monsieur Fouad."

"Where is he now?"

She turned to the Police Superintendent.

"In his room."

She was talking aggressively.

"Don't you like him?"

"Why should I like him?"

"You arrived at eight this morning. Did you come right into this room?"

"First I went to the kitchen to heat some water on the gas stove and to hang up my coat in the closet."

"Then you opened this door?"

"I always start cleaning here."

"What did you do when you saw the body?"

"I telephoned the police station."

"Without telling Monsieur Fouad?"

"Without telling anyone."

"Why?"

"Because I don't trust people, and above all not the people living in this house."

"Why don't you trust them?"

"Because they aren't normal."

"What do you mean?"

She shrugged her shoulders and added:

"I know what I mean. . . . No one can stop me thinking what I like, can they?"

"While you were waiting for the police, did you go and tell the secretary?"

"No. I went to make my coffee in the kitchen. I don't have time to drink it at home in the morning."

"Did Monsieur Fouad come downstairs?"

"He hardly ever comes down before ten."

"Was he asleep?"

"I tell you I didn't go up."

"And the maid?"

"She's Madame's maid. She didn't have anything to do with the gentleman. Since Madame stayed in bed until twelve or later, nothing stopped her making the most of it."

"What's her name?"

31

"Nelly something. I heard her surname once or twice, but I can't remember it. A Dutch name . . . She's Dutch, like Madame."

"Don't you like her either?"

"Is there anything wrong with that?"

"I see from this photograph that Madame Nahour has two children. Are they in the house?"

"They've never set foot in the house."

"Where do they live?"

"Somewhere on the Riviera, with their nurse."

"Did their parents often go and see them?"

"I have no idea. They traveled a great deal, nearly always separately, but I never asked them where they were going."

The van from the Records Office drew up in front of the garden, and Moers came in with his colleagues.

"Did Monsieur Nahour entertain much?"

"What do you mean by entertain?"

"Did he invite friends to lunch or dinner?"

"Not since I've been here. Anyhow, he usually dined in town."

"And his wife?"

"So did she."

"Together?"

"I never followed them."

"Any visitors?"

"Sometimes Monsieur Nahour would see someone in his office."

"A friend?"

"I don't listen at keyholes. . . . Usually foreigners, people from his country, and he spoke in a language I couldn't understand."

"Was Monsieur Fouad there when these people came?"

"Sometimes he was, sometimes he wasn't."

"Just a minute, Moers . . . You can't begin before the Medical Examiner gets here. . . . Thank you, Madame Bodin. Will you please stay in the kitchen and not do any housework until these premises have been examined. . . . Where is Madame Nahour's room?"

"Upstairs."

"Monsieur Nahour and his wife shared a room, did they?"

"No. Monsieur Nahour's rooms are on the ground floor, on the other side of the corridor."

"Isn't there any dining room?"

"The study was used as a dining room."

"Thank you for your help."

"Don't mention it."

And she went out with dignity.

A moment later Maigret climbed the stairs, covered with a carpet of the same lavender-blue as the floor of the study. Manicle and Lapointe followed him. On the landing they found the local plain-clothes detective smoking a cigarette resignedly.

"Which is Madame Nahour's room?"

"This one, just opposite."

The room was spacious, with Louis XVI furniture. Although the bed hadn't been slept in, it was quite untidy. A green dress and some lingerie lay on the carpet. The doors of the closets were wide open and suggested a hurried departure. Several bare hangers, one on the bed and others on the silk-covered armchair, made it look as though some clothes had been grabbed and stuffed into a suitcase.

Maigret casually opened some drawers.

"Will you call the maid, Lapointe?"

This took some time. Then a young woman, with hair almost as fair as Madame Nahour's, and astonishingly light-blue eyes, appeared in the doorway, followed by Lapointe.

She was not wearing working clothes or the usual black dress and white apron, but a tweed suit, which fitted her very tightly.

She looked like the Dutch girls on chocolate boxes; all she needed was her national bonnet with its two points.

"Come in . . . Sit down . . ."

Her face was blank, as though she didn't understand what was going on or who the people standing in front of her were.

"What's your name?"

She shook her head, but opened her mouth a little and said:

"No understand."

"Can't you speak French?"

She shook her head.

"Only Dutch?"

Maigret was already imagining the complications involved in getting a translator.

"English, too."

"You speak English?"

"Yes."

The little English that Maigret spoke was not enough for an interrogation which might prove important.

"Shall I translate, chief?" suggested Lapointe shyly.

The Superintendent looked at him in surprise, because the young inspector had never told him he could speak English.

"Where did you learn it?"

"I've been studying it for a year."

The girl looked at them in turn. When she was asked a question, she did not answer at once, but took the time to assimilate what she had been told.

She was not aggressively suspicious, like the cleaning woman, but displayed a sort of impassiveness, which might have been natural or acquired. Was she purposely trying to appear well below average in intelligence?

Even in English, the sentences seemed to sink in with difficulty and her replies were brief, elementary.

Her name was Velthuis, she was twenty-four years old, had been born in Friesland in the north of Holland, and had gone to Amsterdam when she was fifteen.

"Did she enter Madame Nahour's service at once?"

Lapointe translated the question, and in reply simply got the word:

"No."

"When did she become her maid?"

"Six years ago."

"How?"

"Through an advertisement in a paper in Amsterdam."

"Was Madame Nahour already married?"

"Yes."

"Since when?"

"She doesn't know."

Maigret had great difficulty in controlling himself,

because with these Nos and Yeses the interrogation could last a long time.

"Tell her I don't like being taken for a fool."

Lapointe translated awkwardly, and the girl looked at the Superintendent in slight surprise before resuming her expression of total indifference.

Two dark cars drew up to the house and Maigret muttered:

"The Public Prosecutor . . . Stay with her, will you? Try to get as much as you can out of her."

The Deputy Public Prosecutor, Noiret, was an elderly man, with an old-fashioned gray goatee, who had served in most of the provincial law courts and had finally been appointed to Paris, where he was waiting to retire and cautiously avoiding all difficulties.

The Medical Examiner, a certain Collinet, who was leaning over the body, had replaced Doctor Paul, with whom Maigret had worked for so many years. Other men had also disappeared as time went by, like the Magistrate, Coméliau, whom Maigret could call his intimate enemy and sometimes even missed.

As for the Magistrate, Cayotte, who was relatively young, he always let the police work for two or three days on a case before having anything to do with it himself.

The doctor had twice changed the position of the body, and his hands were sticky with clotted blood. He looked around for Maigret.

"Of course, I can't tell you anything definite before the post-mortem. The position of the bullet hole makes me think it was a weapon of medium or large caliber, which was fired at a distance of over two yards.

"Since there's no hole on the other side, the bullet has remained in the body. I can't imagine that it lodged in the throat, where it would not have met with any resistance, so I suppose that, since it was shot upward, it lodged in the skull."

"You mean to say that the victim could have been standing up, while the murderer was sitting on the other side of the desk?"

"Not necessarily sitting, but he could have fired without raising his arm, from the hip."

It wasn't until the ambulance men lifted the body onto a stretcher that a 6.35 revolver with a mother-of-pearl handle was revealed lying on the carpet.

The Deputy and the Magistrate looked at Maigret to see what he thought.

"I don't suppose the wound could have been caused by this weapon, could it?" the Superintendent asked the Medical Examiner.

"I would say no, for the time being."

"Will you examine the pistol, Moers?"

Moers took a rag to pick it up, sniff it, and then to take out the magazine.

"A bullet's missing, chief."

Since the body was being taken away, the men from the Records Office and the photographer could get down to work. The photographer had already taken some pictures of the dead man. Everybody was coming and going. Little groups gathered. The Deputy, Noiret, tugged the Superintendent's sleeve.

"What nationality do you think he was?"

"Lebanese."

"Do you think it's a political crime?"

This prospect scared him, because he could remember similar cases, which had ended pretty badly for everybody concerned.

"I think I'll be able to tell you quite soon."

"Have you questioned the staff?"

"The cleaning woman, who isn't very talkative, and I've asked a few questions of the maid, who's even less so. Admittedly she can't speak a word of French, and Inspector Lapointe's questioning her in English, upstairs."

"Let me know as soon as possible."

He looked for the Magistrate so that they could leave together, because the Public Prosecutor appeared only as a formality.

"You don't need me or my men, do you?" asked the District Superintendent.

"I don't need you, my friend, but it would be a help if you could leave me your detectives for a little longer, as well as the policeman at the door."

"By all means."

The room gradually grew emptier, and Maigret found himself standing in front of a library consisting of over three hundred volumes. He was surprised to see that they were nearly all scientific works, mainly mathematical, and a whole row of books in French and English was devoted to the theory of probability.

Opening the cupboards under the bookshelves, he found them full of papers, some of which were copies, containing columns of figures.

"Don't leave before you've seen me, Moers. . . . Send the gun to Gastine-Renette to get an expert analysis. . . . Incidentally, send this bullet with it."

He took the bullet Pardon had handed him out of his pocket. It was wrapped up in a piece of cotton.

"Where did you find that?"

"I'll tell you later. . . . I'd like to know urgently whether the bullet was shot from this revolver."

Lighting his pipe, he went up the stairs, glanced into the room where Lapointe was sitting opposite the Dutch girl and taking notes on a pad that he rested on the dressing table.

"Where's the secretary?" he asked the local detective who was hanging about in the hallway.

"The door at the end."

"Has he been complaining?"

"He occasionally opens his door and listens. He had a telephone call."

"What did the Superintendent say to him this morning?"

"That his boss had been murdered and that he wasn't to leave his room until further orders."

"Were you there?"

"Yes."

"Did he look surprised?"

"He's not the sort of man who shows his feelings. You'll see for yourself."

Maigret knocked at the same time as he turned the door handle and pushed the door open. The room was tidy, and if the bed had been slept in that night, it had been carefully remade. Nothing was out of place. There was a small desk in front of the window, a fawn-colored leather armchair near the desk, and, from the armchair, a man watched the Superintendent come into the room.

It was difficult to tell exactly how old he was. He

looked very Arabic, his skin was dark, and his face, in spite of its lines, could just as well have been that of a man of forty as of a man of sixty. His hair was thick, pitch-black, without a trace of white.

He did not get up, made no move to greet his visitor, merely looked at him with his smoldering eyes without betraying any feeling.

"I suppose you speak French?"

He nodded.

"I'm Superintendent Maigret, head of the Crime Squad. I assume you are Monsieur Nahour's secretary?"

Another nod.

"May I ask your full name?"

"Fouad Oueni."

The voice was hoarse, as though he suffered from chronic laryngitis.

"Are you aware of what happened last night in the study?"

"No."

"But you were told that Monsieur Nahour was killed."

"No more than that."

"Where were you?"

Not a feature quivered. Maigret had rarely met with so little co-operation as when he had entered this house. The cleaning woman only answered questions evasively, with hostility. The Dutch maid simply replied in monosyllables.

As for Fouad Oueni, who was wearing a very neat black suit, a white shirt, and a dark-gray tie, he watched and listened to the Superintendent with total indifference, almost with disdain.

40

"Did you spend the night in this room?"

"After half past one this morning."

"You mean you came in at half past one this morning?"

"I thought you'd gathered that."

"Where were you until then?"

"At the Saint-Michel Club."

"A gambling club?"

The man simply shrugged his shoulders.

"Where exactly is it?"

"Above the Bar des Tilleuls."

"Did you gamble?"

"No."

"What did you do?"

"I made a note of the winning numbers."

Was it irony that gave him that self-satisfied look? Maigret sat on a chair and went on asking questions as though he were unaware of the other man's hostility.

"Was the light on in the study when you came in?"

"I don't know."

"Were the curtains drawn?"

"I suppose so. They are drawn every night."

"You didn't see a light under the door?"

"One can never see a light under that door."

"Was Monsieur Nahour usually in bed at that hour?"

"That depended."

"On what?"

"On him."

"Did he often go out at night?"

"When he wanted to."

"Where did he go?"

"Wherever he liked."

"Alone?"

"He left the house alone."

"By car?"

"He called a taxi."

"Didn't he drive himself?"

"He didn't like driving. In the daytime I was his chauffeur."

"What sort of car has he got?"

"A Bentley."

"Is it in the garage?"

"I'm not sure. I haven't been allowed out of my room."

."And Madame Nahour?"

"What about her?"

"Did she have a car, too?"

"A green Triumph."

"Did she go out yesterday evening?"

"I never had anything to do with her."

"What time did you leave the house?"

"Half past ten."

"Was she here?"

"I don't know."

"And Monsieur Nahour?"

"I don't know if he was back. He must have dined in town."

"Do you know where?"

"Probably at the Petit Beyrouth, where he usually dined."

"Who does the cooking in this house?"

"Nobody and everybody."

"How about breakfast?"

"I made it for Monsieur Felix."

"Who is Monsieur Felix?"

"Monsieur Nahour."

"Why do you call him Monsieur Felix?"

"Because there's Monsieur Maurice, too."

"Who is Monsieur Maurice?"

"Monsieur Nahour's father."

"Does he live here?"

"No. In Lebanon."

"And then?"

"Monsieur Pierre, Monsieur Felix's brother."

"Where does he live?"

"In Geneva."

"Who telephoned you this morning?"

"Nobody telephoned me."

"But the telephone was heard ringing in your room."

"I'd asked for Geneva and they called me back when they had the number."

"Monsieur Pierre?"

"Yes."

"Did you tell him what happened?"

"I told him Monsieur Felix was dead. Monsieur Pierre will be at Orly in a few minutes, because he took the first plane."

"Do you know what he does in Geneva?"

"He's a banker."

"And Monsieur Maurice Nahour in Beirut?"

"He's a banker."

"And Monsieur Felix?"

"He had no profession."

"Have you been working for him long?"

"I wasn't working for him."

"Didn't you work as his secretary? You just told me you cooked his breakfast and worked as his chauffeur."

"I helped him."

"Since when?"

"Eighteen years ago."

"Did you know him in Beirut?"

"I met him at law school."

"In Paris?"

He nodded, impassive and stiff in his armchair, while Maigret was getting impatient.

"Did he have any enemies?"

"Not as far as I know."

"Did he meddle in politics?"

"Certainly not."

"So you went out at half past ten without knowing who was in the house. You went to a gambling club on Boulevard Saint-Michel where you noted the winning numbers but did not gamble yourself. Then you came back at half past one and came up here still without knowing where anybody was. Is that right? You saw nothing, heard nothing, and you didn't expect to be waked up this morning with the news that Monsieur Nahour had been shot."

"You're the first person to tell me a firearm was used."

"What do you know about Felix Nahour's family?"

"Nothing. It's none of my business."

"Was it a happy marriage?"

"I don't know."

"You give me the impression that the husband and the wife didn't see much of each other."

"I think that's quite common."

"Why don't the children live in Paris?"

"Maybe they prefer the Riviera."

"Where did Monsieur Nahour live before he rented this house?"

"All over the place . . . Italy . . . A year in Cuba before the revolution . . . We also had a villa in Deauville."

"Do you often go to the Saint-Michel Club?"

"Two or three times a week."

"And you never gamble?"

"Rarely."

"Will you come down with me?"

When he stood up, Fouad Oueni looked even thinner than he had looked in his chair. They went down the stairs.

"How old are you?"

"I don't know. In the mountains where I was born there was no such thing as a registry office. The age on my passport is fifty-one."

"Are you older or younger?"

"I don't know."

In the study Moers's men were putting away their equipment.

When the van drove off and the two men were alone together, Maigret asked:

"Look around the room and tell me if anything's missing. Or if something's been added."

Oueni tore himself away from the patch of blood he was gazing at, opened the right-hand drawer in the desk, and said:

"The revolver's gone."

"What type?"

"A Browning 6.35."

"With a mother-of-pearl handle?"

"Yes."

"Why did Felix Nahour have a gun that is usually regarded as likely to belong to a woman?"

"It used to belong to Madame Nahour."

"How long ago?"

"I don't know."

"Did he take it away from her?"

"He didn't tell me."

"Did he have a license?"

"He never carried this pistol on him."

Regarding the matter as settled, the Lebanese opened the other drawers, which contained some files, and then went toward the bookshelves and opened the doors below.

"Can you tell me what these lists of figures are?"

Oueni looked at him in astonishment mingled with irony, as though Maigret should have understood by himself.

"They're the winning numbers in the main casinos. The typed lists are sent by agencies to their subscribers. Monsieur Felix got the others from a croupier."

Maigret was about to ask another question, but Lapointe appeared in the doorway.

"Will you come up a minute, chief?"

"Something new?"

"Not much, but I think you ought to know."

"I must ask you not to leave the building without my permission, Monsieur Oueni."

"Can I make myself some coffee?"

Maigret shrugged his shoulders and turned on his heel.

❧ 3 ❧

MAIGRET HAD RARELY FELT SO MUCH OUT OF HIS ELEMENT, so far from normal life, with that feeling of ill-ease we have when we dream that the ground has slipped away from under our feet.

In the snow-covered streets the few passers-by walked along trying to keep their balance; the cars, the taxis, the buses drove slowly, while trucks full of sand or salt drove along the edge of the sidewalk at walking pace.

The lights were on in almost every window, and snow still fell from a sky as gray as slate.

He could almost have told what was going on in all these little compartments where human beings were breathing. In the course of over thirty years he had learned to know Paris quarter by quarter, street by street, and yet here he felt immersed in a different world, where people's reactions were unpredictable.

How had Felix Nahour been living a few hours earlier? What exactly was his relationship with his secretary who was not a secretary, with his wife and his two

47

children? Why were the children on the Riviera, and why. . . ?

There were so many whys that he could take only one on at a time. Nothing was clear. Nothing happened as it happened in other families, in other homes.

Pardon had felt just as uneasy the night before when a strange couple had invaded his little office.

The story about a shot fired from a moving car was unlikely, as was the old woman who pointed out the doctor's house.

Felix Nahour, with his works on mathematics and his lists of winning and losing numbers in various casinos, did not fit into any category that Maigret knew of, and Fouad Oueni was also from another world.

Everything here seemed false to him, everyone seemed to be lying, and, as he went up the stairs, Lapointe confirmed his feeling.

"I wonder if this girl is normal, chief. Judging from her answers, when she does answer, and from the way she looks at me, she seems to have the ingenuousness and mentality of a child of ten, but I wonder if it isn't a trick, or a game."

As they went into Madame Nahour's room, where Nelly was still sitting on a silk-upholstered chair, Lapointe said:

"By the way, chief, the children are no longer as young as they were when that picture was taken. The girl's now five and the little boy two."

"Do you know where they live with their nurse?"

"In Mougins, Pension des Palmiers."

"Since when?"

"As far as I can gather, the boy was born in Cannes and has never been to Paris."

48

The maid looked at them with her light, transparent blue eyes, appearing not to understand a word they were saying.

"I found more photographs in a drawer she pointed out to me. A dozen snapshots of the children as babies, then walking, and this one, taken on the beach, of Nahour and his wife, far younger, probably at the time when they met . . . Here's a later photograph of Madame Nahour, with a friend, near a canal in Amsterdam."

The friend was ugly, with a flat nose and tiny eyes, but nevertheless she had a pleasant open face.

"The only letters in the room are from a girl, in Dutch. They have been written over about seven years and the last one is dated ten days ago."

"Has Nelly ever been to Holland with her mistress?"

"She says not."

"Does Madame Nahour go there often?"

"Occasionally . . . By herself, apparently . . . But I'm not quite sure whether Nelly really understands my questions, even in English."

"Get a translator for these letters . . . What does she say about yesterday evening and last night?"

"Nothing. She doesn't know anything. The house isn't that big, and yet nobody seems to know what anybody else does. She thinks Madame Nahour dined in town."

"Alone? Didn't someone pick her up? Didn't she call a taxi?"

"She says she doesn't know."

"Didn't she help Madame Nahour dress?"

"She says that she didn't ring for her. . . . She ate in the kitchen as usual, and then she went up to her room, read a Dutch newspaper, and went to bed. . . . She showed me the newspaper, which is dated the day before yesterday."

"Didn't she hear any steps in the hall?"

"She didn't take any notice of them. Once she's asleep nothing seems to wake her."

"What time does she start work in the morning?"

"No definite time."

Maigret tried vainly to make out what was going on behind the ivorylike forehead of the maid, who was smiling at him vaguely.

"Tell her she can go and have breakfast, but that she isn't allowed to leave the house."

When Lapointe had translated these instructions, Nelly got up, curtsied like a little girl, and walked quietly toward the staircase.

"She's lying, chief."

"How do you know?"

"She says she didn't come into this room last night. This morning the local detective didn't let her out of her room. And yet the first time I asked her what coat her mistress was wearing, she didn't hesitate to say:

" 'The seal one.'

"Well, the closets were closed, and in one of them I found a mink coat and in the other a gray astrakhan. . . ."

"I would like you to take the car and go to see Doctor Pardon on Boulevard Voltaire. Show him the photograph on the desk downstairs . . ."

There was a telephone in the room. When it started ringing Maigret picked up the receiver and heard two voices—the Medical Examiner and Oueni.

"Yes," said Oueni. "He's still here. . . . Wait a minute. . . . I'll tell him. . . ."

"You needn't do that, Monsieur Oueni," Maigret interrupted. "Would you mind hanging up, please."

So the three telephones, including the secretary's, were hooked together.

"Hello, this is Maigret. . . ."

"This is Collinet. I've only just started the post-mortem, but I thought you'd like to know the first result immediately. . . . It wasn't suicide."

"I never thought it would be."

"Nor did I, but now we're sure. . . . Although I'm not an expert on guns, I can tell you that the bullet I've found in the skull was fired from a medium- or large-caliber gun, a 7.32 or 7.45, as I expected. I'd say it was fired at about three or four yards' range, and the skull has been split. . . ."

"What time did he die?"

"To be sure about that I'd have to know the time of his last meal and analyze his internal organs. . . ."

"Roughly?"

"About midnight."

"Thank you, doctor."

Lapointe had gone out, and his car could be heard in the street.

Downstairs two men were talking in a foreign language the Superintendent finally recognized as Arabic. He went down and found Oueni standing in the hall talking to someone he had not seen before, and the local detective, who was looking on, not daring to interrupt.

51

The newcomer looked like Felix Nahour, a little older, a little thinner, and also taller. His dark hair was growing gray at the temples.

"Monsieur Pierre Nahour?"

"Are you from the police?" he asked suspiciously.

"Superintendent Maigret, head of the Crime Squad."

"What's happened to my brother? Where's the body?"

"He was killed by a bullet in his throat last night, and his body has been taken to the Medico-Legal Institute. . . ."

"Will I be able to see him?"

"Later."

"Why not now?"

"Because the post-mortem is being performed. . . . Come in, Monsieur Nahour."

He hesitated about whether to let Oueni into the study, then made up his mind:

"Will you wait in your room?"

Oueni and Nahour looked at each other, and Maigret could see no sign of sympathy in the newcomer's eyes.

When the door was shut, the banker from Geneva asked:

"What's happened?"

The Superintendent pointed to the large patch of blood on the carpet, and the other man drew back an instant, as he would have done in the presence of a body.

"How did that happen?"

"Nobody knows. He apparently dined in town, and nobody saw him afterward."

"How about Lina?"

"Do you mean Madame Nahour? . . . Her maid claims

that she dined out, too, and that she isn't back yet."

"Isn't she here?"

"Her bed hasn't been slept in and she's taken her luggage."

Pierre Nahour did not look surprised.

"And Oueni?"

"He says he went to a gambling club on Boulevard Saint-Michel and noted the winning numbers until one in the morning. When he came back he didn't look to see whether his boss was in and went to bed. He didn't hear anything."

They were sitting opposite each other, and the banker had automatically pulled a cigar out of his pocket, which he hesitated to light, maybe out of respect for the dead man, although he was no longer there.

"I must ask you certain questions, Monsieur Nahour, and I beg you to forgive my indiscretion. Were you on good terms with your brother?"

"On very good terms, although we did not see each other frequently."

"Why not?"

"Because I live in Geneva, and when I travel it's usually to go to Lebanon. . . . As for my brother, he had no reason to come to Geneva. It wasn't one of his centers of activity."

"Oueni told me that Felix Nahour did not have any profession."

"Yes and no . . . Look, Monsieur Maigret, before you ask any more questions I think I ought to give you some information that will enable you to understand that situation. . . . My father was, and still is, a banker in Beirut. To start with he had a very small firm that

53

was mainly intended to finance imports and exports, because all products on their way to the Near East pass through Beirut. In Beirut there are more banks in proportion to the population than anywhere else. . . ."

He finally made up his mind to light his cigar. His hands were as well manicured as his brother's and he was also wearing a wedding ring.

"We are Maronite Christians, which accounts for our Christian names. . . . My father's concern expanded over the years, and he now directs one of the most important private banks in Lebanon. . . .

"I studied at the law school in Paris, and then at the Institute of Comparative Law."

"Before your brother arrived?"

"He's five years younger than I. So I was ahead of him. When he arrived I had almost finished my studies."

"Did you settle in Geneva immediately?"

"First I worked with my father, and then we decided to open a Swiss branch, the Comptoir Libanais, which I direct. It's a fairly small concern, with five employees and offices on the second floor of a building on Avenue du Rhône."

Now that he was faced with a man who spoke to him at least with apparent clarity Maigret tried to fit every character into place.

"Have you any other brothers?"

"Only a sister, whose husband directs the same sort of bank as I do, in Istanbul."

"So that your father, your brother-in-law, and you control a large part of the commerce of Lebanon?"

"Let's say a quarter, or even less, a fifth."

"And your brother did not go into the family business?"

54

"He was the youngest. . . . He also started studying law, but without much enthusiasm, and he spent most of his time in the brasseries near the university. . . . He had just discovered poker, at which he turned out to be very good, and he spent whole nights playing it."

"Is that when he met Oueni?"

"I'm not saying that Oueni, who isn't a Maronite but a Moslem, was his evil genius, but I'm not far off thinking so. . . . Oueni was very poor, like most people from the mountains. He had to work to pay for his studies."

"So I'm right in understanding, from certain discoveries I've made in this room, that your brother was a professional gambler . . .?"

"As far as one can call that a profession. One day we heard that he'd stopped studying law and was following a course in mathematics at the Sorbonne. . . . His father and he were at daggers drawn for several years."

"And you?"

"I saw him from time to time. . . . To begin with, I had to lend him some money."

"Which he paid back?"

"Every penny. You mustn't think that my brother was a failure. The first months, the first two or three years, were difficult, but he was soon winning large sums of money, and I'm sure he became richer than I."

"Did he make it up with his father?"

"Quite quickly . . . We Maronites have a very strong family feeling."

"I suppose your brother gambled mainly in casinos?"

"In Deauville, Cannes, Evian, in Enghien in the winter. For one or two years, before Castro, he was technical adviser and, I should imagine, an associate of the casino in Havana. . . . He didn't gamble haphazardly, but used his mathematical education."

"Are you married, Monsieur Nahour?"

"Married and have four children, one of whom is twenty-one and studies at Harvard."

"When did your brother get married?"

"Just a minute . . . It was in . . . It was seven years ago. . . ."

"Do you know his wife?"

"Of course I've met Lina."

"Did you meet her before her marriage?"

"No . . . We all had the impression that my brother was a confirmed bachelor."

"How did you hear about his marriage?"

"From a letter . . ."

"Do you know where they were married?"

"At Trouville, where Felix had rented a villa."

Pierre Nahour's face had grown slightly darker.

"What sort of a woman is she?"

"I don't know what to say."

"Why?"

"Because I've seen her only twice."

"Did your brother take her to Geneva?"

"No. I came to Paris on business and I met them both at the Ritz, where they were living at the time."

"Didn't your brother ever go to Lebanon with her?"

"No. My father met them a few months later in Evian, where he was taking a cure."

"Did your father approve of the marriage?"

"I can't answer for my father."

"Did you?"

"It was none of my business."

It had all become imprecise again, with vague or equivocal replies.

"Do you know where your brother met the woman who was later to be his wife?"

"He never told me, but it was quite easy to guess. The year before, the Miss Europe beauty contest was supposed to take place in Deauville. Felix was there because there were some very big games at the casino, and the bank was losing almost every evening. . . . A Dutch girl of nineteen won the contest, Lina Wiemers."

"Whom your brother married . . ."

"About a year later . . . Before the marriage they traveled a great deal, the two of them, or, rather, the three of them, because Felix never moved without Fouad Oueni."

They were interrupted by the telephone. Maigret picked up the receiver. Lapointe was on the line.

"I'm calling you from Doctor Pardon's apartment, chief. . . . He recognized the photograph at once. . . . It is the woman he saw last night."

"Will you come back here? Pass by Quai des Orfèvres on your way and ask Janvier, if he's there, or else Torrence or somebody, to join me on Avenue du Parc-Montsouris with a car."

He hung up.

"I'm sorry, Monsieur Nahour. . . . I have a more indiscreet question to ask you, and you'll soon know why. . . . Do you know if your brother and his wife got on well together?"

Pierre Nahour's face suddenly seemed to close.

"I'm afraid I can't tell you anything. . . . I never had anything to do with my brother's married life."

"His room was on this floor and his wife's on the floor above. . . . As far as I can gather from more than reluctant information, they did not have their meals together and rarely went out together."

Pierre Nahour did not flinch, but his cheeks turned slightly pinker.

"The staff in this house consists of a cleaning woman, Fouad Oueni, who plays a pretty mysterious part, and a Dutch maid who can speak only Dutch and English."

"Besides Arabic, my brother spoke French, English, Spanish, and Italian, not to mention a little German."

"Oueni cooked breakfast for his master, and Nelly Velthuis did it for her mistress. The same went for lunch, when they lunched here, and they usually dined in town, but separately."

"I wasn't aware of that."

"Where are your children, Monsieur Nahour?"

"But . . . in Geneva, of course, or, rather, seven miles outside Geneva, where we have our villa."

"Your brother's children live on the Riviera with a governess."

"Felix frequently went to see them, and he spent part of the year in Cannes."

"And his wife?"

"I suppose she went to see them, too."

"Have you ever heard that she had one or more lovers?"

"I don't frequent the same set."

"Now, Monsieur Nahour, I shall try to reconstruct what happened last night, or what we know about it. . . . Before one o'clock in the morning your brother was hit in the throat by a bullet fired from a revolver

58

of fairly large caliber, and we shall know the type and probably the make as soon as the expert sends us his report. . . . At that moment he was standing behind his desk.

"Well, your brother, like his aggressor, had a gun in his hand, a 6.35 pistol with a mother-of-pearl handle, which was usually in the right-hand drawer of his desk, a drawer we found half open. . . .

"I have no idea how many people were in the room, but we know your sister-in-law was here."

"How can you know that?"

"Because she was wounded by a bullet fired from a 6.35. Have you ever heard of a certain Doctor Pardon who lives on Boulevard Voltaire?"

"I don't know the district and I've never heard that name before."

"Your sister-in-law must have heard of it, or else the man who was with her. . . ."

"You mean there was another man in this study?"

"I'm almost sure. . . . Before or after the scene that I've just described, Madame Nahour quickly piled some lingerie and clothes into one or more suitcases. Shortly after, wearing a sealskin coat, she and her companion got out of a red Alfa Romeo in front of 76b Boulevard Voltaire, and a little later they rang at Doctor Pardon's door."

"Who was the man?"

"All we know is that he's a Colombian citizen, twenty-five or -six years old."

Pierre Nahour did not flinch, had not even quivered.

"Have you any idea who he could be?" asked Maigret, looking him in the eye.

"None," he said, taking the cigar out of his mouth.

"Your sister-in-law had a wound in her back but it was not fatal. Doctor Pardon dressed it. The Colombian told an absurd story, according to which his companion, whom he did not know, was attacked a short distance away from him by one or more individuals who fired from the door of a car."

"Where is she?"

"In all likelihood in Amsterdam . . . While the doctor was washing his hands and taking off his bloodstained coat the couple crept out of his office. . . . Some time later they appeared at Orly, where the red car is still parked. A Dutch woman and a Colombian, answering to the description of the doctor's patient and her escort, got on the plane to Amsterdam."

Maigret stood up and emptied his pipe in an ashtray before filling another one, which he pulled out of his pocket.

"I've put my cards on the table, Monsieur Nahour. . . . I expect you to be just as frank with me. . . . I'm going back to my office on Quai des Orfèvres. One of my detectives is staying in this building to make sure that neither the cleaning woman, nor Oueni, nor Nelly leaves without my permission."

"How about me?"

"I would like you to stay here, too, because as soon as the post-mortem is over I shall ask you to identify the body. This is only a formality, but an indispensable formality."

He went over to the bay window. It was still snowing, more lightly, but the sky was no brighter. Two black cars from the Police Judiciaire drew up along the sidewalk.

60

Lapointe got out of one and Janvier out of the other. They crossed the garden, and then the door could be heard opening in the hallway.

"When we see each other again, Monsieur Nahour, you may be able to tell me more about the relationship between your sister-in-law and your brother, and perhaps even about her and other men. . . ."

Pierre Nahour did not reply.

"You stay here, Lapointe. . . . I'm going to the Quai with Janvier."

And Maigret wound his thick scarf around his neck and put on his overcoat.

It was ten to twelve when Maigret, sunk in his armchair, finally got his call to Amsterdam.

"Keulemans? . . . Hello. This is Maigret, in Paris. . . ."

The head of the Crime Squad in Amsterdam, Jef Keulemans, was still young, hardly forty, and he looked about ten years younger because of his tall boyish figure, his pink face, and his fair hair.

When he had come to work for a time in Paris, it was Maigret who had shown him the inner workings of the Police Judiciare, and the two men had become good friends, occasionally seeing each other again at international congresses.

"Very well, thank you, Keulemans . . . My wife, too . . . What? . . . The port's covered with ice? . . . Here, too. Paris is like a skating rink and it's starting to snow again.

"Look, I want to ask you for a favor. . . . I'm sorry I'm only calling you for that. . . . It's official, of course. . . . To start with, I haven't got time to fill in the documents necessary to go through official channels. And then, I haven't got enough information. . . .

"Last night two people who interest me took a KLM flight that left Orly at about four in the morning. . . . A man and a woman. They may have pretended not to be together. . . . The man has a Colombian passport and is about twenty-five. The woman is of Dutch origin, is named Evelina Nahour, maiden name Wiemars, and pays brief visits to Amsterdam, where she spent her late teens. . . .

"I suppose they both filled in landing cards which you can find at the airport. . . .

"Madame Nahour does not reside in Holland, but she has a friend in Amsterdam, Anna Keegel, who gives an address on Lomanstraat on the back of her letters. . . . You know it? . . .

"Good . . . No, don't arrest them . . . But if you see the Nahour woman, maybe you could just tell her that her husband is dead and that she is needed for the reading of the will. . . . Tell her her brother-in-law is in Paris. . . . Don't mention the police.

"Nahour has been murdered, yes. . . . A bullet in his throat . . . What? . . . She probably knows, but maybe she doesn't, because I'm ready for every sort of surprise in this case. . . .

"I don't want her to be antagonized. . . . If she's still with her companion, don't bother him. If they've separated, I suppose she'll telephone him and tell him about your call. . . .

"That's good of you, Keulemans. . . . I'm going home for lunch and I'll expect your call this afternoon. . . . Thanks."

Since he had a line, he dialed his own number.

"What have you got for lunch?" he asked when his wife answered the telephone.

"I've cooked some sauerkraut, but I thought I'd have to heat it up this evening, or tomorrow!"

"I'll be back in half an hour."

He took one of the pipes standing on his desk and filled it as he walked slowly down the hall. When he had nearly reached the end, he knocked on Superintendent Lardois's door. Lardois was the head of the Gambling Squad: he had joined the Police Judiciaire at almost the same time as Maigret, and they had been on Christian-name terms from the start.

"Good morning, Raoul."

"How can you remember me? . . . Our offices are twenty yards apart and you don't even look in once a year."

"I could say the same about you."

Nevertheless, they saw each other in an official capacity every morning at the report session in the Chief of the Police Judiciaire's office.

"You may think I'm naïve, but I don't know anything about gambling. . . . To start with, are there such things as professional gamblers?"

"Casino managers are, since they are really playing against the guests. When they're holding a double bank they sometimes go halves with a gambling expert, and sometimes with a group. . . . So much for the professionals, who've got an establishment of their own.

"Other people, not many of them, live off gambling alone for a certain amount of time, either because they're exceptionally lucky or because they have large financial means and are particularly good at it."

"Can one gamble scientifically?"

"Apparently. A few players are able to make highly complicated calculations of probability between the deal and the choice of a card."

"Have you heard of a certain Felix Nahour?"

"All the croupiers in France and elsewhere know him. He belongs to the second category, although he used to run an open bank in Havana with an American group."

"Was he honest?"

"If he wasn't, he'd have been a marked man some time ago and he wouldn't be allowed in any casino. . . . It's only in the small casinos that you get seedy-looking cheats, who all get caught sooner or later."

"What do you know about Nahour?"

"First, that he's got a very pretty wife, a Miss Something, whom I've seen several times in Cannes and Biarritz. . . . Then, that he once worked for a group from the Near east . . ."

"A group of gamblers?"

"If you like . . . Let's say gamblers who don't want to, or can't, gamble themselves. . . A professional playing against the bank in Cannes or Deauville, for instance, must have enough millions to continue until his luck is in. Otherwise he has to be on an equal footing with the casino, which has almost inexhaustible resources.

"Hence the formation of groups that work like financial companies, except that they're more discreet.

"For a long time a South American group sent an

operator to Deauville every year, and the bank often found itself in a very nasty position."

"Does Nahour still have a group behind him?"

"Apparently he can fly with his own wings now, but there's no way of finding out."

"One more question . . . Do you know the Saint-Michel Club?"

Lardois hesitated before replying:

"Yes . . . I've raided it a couple of times."

"Why is it still functioning?"

"Don't tell me Nahour plays there?"

"No, but his factotum-secretary spends part of the night there two or three times a week. . . ."

"I turn a blind eye to it for the sake of general information. . . . Most of the guests are foreign students, Orientals who live in the district. . . . It's a good place to keep an eye on them, and our colleagues don't miss their chance. . . . Has there been a row there?"

"No."

"Anything else?"

"No."

"Has Nahour been in trouble?"

"He was murdered last night."

"At a club?"

"At home."

"Will you tell me about it?"

"When I know something myself."

Twenty minutes later Maigret was sitting opposite his wife eating a tasty Alsatian sauerkraut the likes of which can be found in only two restaurants in Paris. The pickled pork was particularly good, and the

Superintendent had opened two bottles of Strasbourg beer.

Beyond the windows the snow was still falling, and it was good to be indoors, in the warmth, and not to have to walk along sidewalks as slippery as the port of Amsterdam.

"Tired?"

"Not particularly."

After a pause he added, with a slightly bantering look at his wife:

"A detective shouldn't really get married."

"So as not to have to go home and eat sauerkraut?" she answered smartly.

"No. Because he ought to live in every social sphere, to know about casinos, for instance, international banking, Lebanese Maronites and Moslems, foreign bistros in the Latin Quarter and Saint-Germain, as well as young Colombians. Not to mention the Dutch language and beauty contests . . ."

"You're getting on all right, aren't you?"

She smiled, because he was gradually looking less worried.

"The rest of the investigation will tell. . . ."

When he got up he felt heavy, but it was because he had indulged in too much lunch and beer. It would have been wonderful to lie in bed, after an almost sleepless night, to have a short siesta and remain vaguely conscious of Madame Maigret moving around the apartment.

"Are you leaving already?"

"Keulemans is calling me from Amsterdam. . . ."

She knew him, too, because he had dined with them several times.

Maigret called a taxi and waited for it, as usual, on the sidewalk.

Janvier had come back to the office.

"Any calls for me?"

"Only Lapointe. Since there wasn't anything to eat in the refrigerator, Nahour's brother asked him if he could have some lunch sent around from a nearby caterer. Lapointe didn't see why he should refuse, and as a reward he was invited to share the meal. The two local detectives went back to the police station. The guard at the door was changed. . . . Oh, I forgot! . . . The young maid didn't want to touch the meal and heated up a mug of chocolate, into which she dipped some crackers."

"Did Nahour and Oueni eat at the same table?"

"Lapointe didn't tell me."

"Go to Boulevard Saint-Michel. There's a place called Bar des Tilleuls, which has a gambling casino disguised as a private club on the second floor. The club's shut at the moment, and you have to go through the bar to get there. . . .

"Tell the owner that Lardois sent you and that we don't want to get him into any trouble. . . . Just try to find out whether Fouad Oueni went to the club last night, and if he did, what time he arrived and what time he left. . . .

"On your way back pass by a restaurant called Petit Beyrouth on Rue des Bernardins. The owner is named Boutros. Felix Nahour was one of his most regular patrons. Did he dine there last night? Was he alone? When did he last go there with his wife? Was there a time when the couple seemed inseparable? And so on . . . See what you can get out of him."

Maigret had not had time to read his morning's mail, which was piling up on his blotter, next to his pipes. He put out his hand to take a letter, yawned, decided to do it later, and, sliding back into his chair, he dropped his head and shut his eyes.

When the telephone made him start, nobody was shaking him by the shoulder and he didn't have to struggle, but the clock said half past three.

"Superintendent Maigret? . . ."

"Hello . . . This is Superintendent Maigret speaking."

The operator had a strong accent.

"This is Amsterdam. Just a minute. I'll connect you with Superintendent Keulemans."

Two or three clicks, then the Dutch detective's cheerful voice.

"Maigret? . . . Keulemans speaking. I wish you'd always give me such easy jobs. . . . Of course I found the landing cards at the airport. I didn't even have to move. They dictated their contents to me on the phone. . . . The woman is indeed Evelina Nahour, maiden name Wiemars, resident of Paris, Avenue du Parc-Montsouris. . . . She's twenty-seven . . . born in Amsterdam, but she left with her parents when she was very young, when her father became assistant manager for a cheesemaker in Leeuwarden, in Friesland."

"Have you seen her?"

"She's staying with her friend, Anna Keegel. The two women lived together for several years when Lina got her parents' permission to work in Amsterdam at the age of seventeen.

"Lina was a switchboard operator for a travel agency, then a receptionist for a well-known doctor, and finally

68

a model for a dress designer. . . . Anna Keegel has always had the same job: secretary in a large brewery. I pointed out its warehouses to you when we sailed down the Amstel together. . . ."

"How did Lina Nahour react when you told her about her husband's death?"

"To start with, she's in bed, and the doctor had just seen her."

"Did she mention her wound to you?"

"No. She said she was very tired."

"Any trace of her companion?"

"Since the apartment consists of only a large room, a kitchen, and a bathroom, I would have seen him. . . . After a pause, she asked:

" 'What did he die of?'

"I said I didn't know, but that she had to be there before they could read the will."

"What did she say?"

"That she hoped to be well enough to take the plane tomorrow morning, although the doctor had said she needed a long rest. . . . I left one of my men stationed in the neighborhood just in case. . . . Officially, don't worry . . ."

"And the Colombian?"

"Vicente Alvaredo, twenty-six years old, born in Bogotá, is a student, resident of Paris, on Rue Notre-Dame-des-Champs . . ."

"Did you find him?"

"Easily. Very officially, too, because I had the telephone of the apartment on Lomanstraat tapped. . . . Lina Nahour picked up the receiver before I had left the street. She dialed the Rembrandt Hotel and was connected with Alvaredo. . . . I've got the shorthand report of their conversation in front of me. Shall I read it to you?"

Maigret was sorry that he couldn't hold the receiver and fill his pipe at the same time and he looked longingly at the tempting row on his desk.

"Here it is:

" 'Vicente?'

" 'Yes. Has the doctor been?'

" 'Half an hour ago. He believed what I told him and he put some stitches in after cleaning the wound. He's coming back tomorrow morning. . . . I had another visit, someone from the police, a very tall and very nice man who told me my husband has died.' "

A pause.

"Note that the young man didn't ask any questions, Maigret.

" 'The lawyer needs me for the reading of the will. I promised to take the plane tomorrow morning.'

" 'Do you think you'll be able to?'

" 'I've only got a temperature of 100.4. . . . Since the doctor gave me some pills, I've hardly felt any pain.'

" 'Can I come and see you this afternoon?'

" 'Not too early, because I want to sleep. My friend called her office to say she had the flu. . . . Apparently a third of the staff's in bed. . . . She's taking good care of me.'

" 'I'll be there at about five.' "

Another pause.

"That's all, Maigret. They started talking in English and then went on in French. Can I do anything else?"

"I'd like to know if she's taking the plane and at what

time she gets to Orly, if she goes. . . . Of course, I'd also like news of Alvaredo."

"Officially!"

And Keulemans ended the conversation gaily, saying, like Maigret's colleagues:

"Good-bye, *chief!*"

❧ 4 ❧

IT WAS AN IDLE AFTERNOON IN AN OVERHEATED OFFICE, AND the six or seven pipes standing on the desk lasted Maigret until he went home. At one point, almost every investigation has what Maigret would call a gap, a point when one has a certain number of elements that must be checked but that cannot yet be put into place.

It is both a peaceful and an irritating period, because there is a temptation to form theories and to draw conclusions, which often turn out to be false.

If Maigret had followed his inclination, if he had not repeated to himself that it was not a Superintendent's job to rush off in every direction like a hunting dog, he would have seen to the whole thing on his own, as he had done when he was still an inspector.

For example, he envied Keuleman's having seen Lina Nahour in the apartment in Amsterdam where she had once lived.

At the same time he would have liked to spend all day, in Lapointe's stead, in the house on Avenue du

Parc-Montsouris, nosing about, sniffing in the corners, opening drawers at random, watching Fouad Oueni, Pierre Nahour, the baffling Nelly, who was maybe not as infantile as she was trying to make believe.

He was not following any preconceived plan. He was going straight ahead, haphazardly, trying, above all, not to make up his mind.

He smiled when there was a knock at the door and he saw Pardon's maid come in.

"Good afternoon, Monsieur Maigret."

Because, for her, he was not the Superintendent of the Police Judiciaire, but the guest who came to dinner every month.

"Here's the statement. The doctor told me to deliver it to you in person."

It was typed with two fingers on the doctor's old typewriter, and there were crossings-out, letters missing, and words run together.

Had Pardon started writing it the night before, after Maigret had left? Or had he written a few lines at a time, between patients? The Superintendent simply looked it over, smiled even more at the care his friend had taken not to omit a single detail, as though it were a medical report.

He soon frowned, however, because he was told that several newspapermen were waiting for him in the hallway. He hesitated, and finally muttered:

"Let them in . . . "

There were five of them, and two photographers, and one of the reporters was young Maquille, who was just twenty, but, despite his cherubic face, was one of the keenest men of the Paris press.

"What can you tell us about the Nahour case?"

Ah! So it was already the Nahour case, a headline in every paper.

"Not much, boys, because it's only just started."

"Do you think Nahour committed suicide?"

"Certainly not. We have proof to the contrary, because the bullet that lodged in the skull after passing through his throat was not shot from the gun found under the body."

"So he was holding a gun when he was killed?"

"Probably. Since I know what you're going to ask next, let me tell you at once that I have no idea who was in the room just then."

"And in the house?" asked young Maquille.

"A young Dutch maid, Nelly Velthuis, was asleep on the second floor in a room fairly far from the study. Apparently she sleeps deeply and she says she heard nothing."

"Wasn't there a secretary, too?"

They must have questioned the neighbors, or even the local shopkeepers.

"Until we receive proof to the contrary, the secretary, Fouad Oueni, was in town and came back at half past one in the morning. He did not go into the study and went straight to bed."

"And Madame Nahour?"

"She'd left."

"Before or after the accident?" asked the obstinate Maquille, always choosing his words well.

"That problem isn't settled yet."

"But it is a problem?"

"There are always problems."

74

"Such as the possibility of a political crime?"

"To the best of our knowledge, Felix Nahour had nothing to do with politics."

"How about his brother in Geneva?"

So they'd got further than the Superintendent had thought.

"Wasn't his bank covering up any other activity?"

"You're going too fast for me."

Nevertheless, Maigret decided to check whether Pierre Nahour had arrived in Paris on the morning flight. So far there was no proof that he had not been in town the day before.

"Had the weapon found under the victim's body been fired?"

And Maigret replied without committing himself:

"It's being examined by the experts and I haven't had a report yet. Now you know about as much as I do, and I want to work. I'll let you know if I hear anything new."

He was aware that Maquille was planning to leave a colleague in the hallway to watch his office and make a note of all his visitors.

"Did . . .?"

"No, boys! I've got a lot to do and I can't spend any more time on you."

That had gone quite well. He sighed and longed for a cold glass of beer, but didn't dare have one sent up from the Brasserie Dauphine.

"Hello? . . . Lapointe? . . . What's going on down there?"

"The house is just as gloomy as ever. The cleaning woman is furious about not being able to get on with her work. Nelly's lying on her bed reading an English detective story. As for Pierre Nahour, he hasn't left the study, where he's going through the correspondence and papers in the drawers."

"Has he made any phone calls?"

"Just one, to Beirut, to tell his father. His father's trying to get on the next flight."

"Can I speak to Pierre Nahour, please?"

"He's next to me."

Then came the voice of the banker from Geneva.

"Yes . . ."

"Do you know if your brother had a lawyer in Paris?"

"Felix mentioned one when we last met, three years ago, and said that if he died his will was with Maître Leroy-Beaulieu on Boulevard Saint-Germain. I happen to know Leroy-Beaulieu very well, because I did part of my law studies with him, but we've been out of touch since then."

"Did your brother tell you what was in his will?"

"No. He only said rather bitterly that, in spite of his father's criticisms, he remained a Nahour."

"Have you found anything in the papers you're looking at?"

"Mainly bills, which show that my sister-in-law had no dealings with the shopkeepers, not even with the butcher or the grocer, and left it all to my brother. Then there are almost daily reports from the nurse giving news of the children, which proves that my brother was very fond of them. Invitations, letters from casino managers and croupiers . . ."

"Look, Monsieur Nahour. There is no need for you to stay indoors. You can go wherever you like in Paris, provided you don't leave the city. If you take a room in a hotel . . ."

"I don't intend to. I'll sleep in my brother's room. I may go out, if only to have dinner."

"May I speak to my inspector again? . . . Hello . . . Lapointe? . . . I've just given Pierre Nahour permission to go wherever he likes. This does not apply to Oueni, and I don't want the maid to leave the house either.

"The cleaning woman can do the shopping and go home, if she likes.

"Toward the end of the afternoon I'll send someone to replace you. See you later . . ."

He went into the detectives' office, where about fifteen of them were at work, some typing out reports, others making telephone calls.

"Can anyone speak fairly good English here?"

They looked at each other in silence; then Baron raised his hand shyly.

"But I've got a bad accent."

"Take over from Lapointe between five and six on Avenue du Parc-Montsouris. He'll give you further instructions. . . ."

When he returned to his office a little later, Maigret found Janvier in his overcoat; he had brought a blast of icy air from outside into the room.

"I've seen the owner of the Bar des Tilleuls, a large sleepy fellow who I suspect is cleverer than he wants to appear. He says he hasn't got anything to do with the club on the second floor, which is run by someone named Pozzi, except that the customers have to pass through the bar. . . .

"Every evening, from eight to eleven or twelve, the

bar is full, because a great many people come to watch television.

"It was particularly crowded last night because there was a volleyball match on. He didn't see Oueni arrive, but he saw him leave at about quarter past one."

"So Oueni could have arrived at any time before quarter past one, and just have stayed a few minutes in the club?"

"That's possible. If you don't mind, I'll go and question Pozzi this evening, as well as the croupiers, and, if necessary, the customers."

Maigret would like to have gone himself. He hesitated to admit that he had better go to bed, after an almost sleepless night, in view of the work he would be faced with the next day.

"How about the restaurant?"

"It's a very small room with such a strong smell of Oriental cooking that it made me dizzy. Boutros is a plump fellow who swings his thick legs as he walks. He apparently didn't know about what had happened last night, because when I told him Nahour was dead he started crying.

" 'My best customer! . . . My brother! . . .' he exclaimed. 'Yes, Inspector, I loved that man like a brother. . . . He used to eat here when he was a student, and I often let him have credit for weeks on end. . . . When he got rich he didn't forget poor Boutros, and when he's in Paris he comes here almost every evening.

" 'That's his table there, in the corner, you see, near the counter. . . .' "

"Did he say anything about Madame Nahour?"

"He's an old fox, too, and he watches one out of the corner of his eye. . . . He raved on and on about Madame Nahour's beauty, her sweetness, her kindness.

" 'And she wasn't proud, Inspector! . . . She'd always shake my hand when she arrived and when she left.' "

"When did he see her last?"

"He doesn't know. . . . He's very vague. . . . 'Shortly after her marriage she used to come more often with her husband than she has recently, yes. . . . They were a handsome couple, very much in love. . . . They've always been very much in love. . . . No, nothing went wrong, but she had to look after the house and the children.' "

"Doesn't he know that the children live on the Riviera?"

"He pretends not to."

Maigret could not suppress a smile. Was everybody lying in this case? It had started with a lie at Pardon's the night before, what with the incredible story about the shot from a car and the old woman who had pointed out the doctor's house.

"Just a minute!" the Superintendent told Janvier. "I must make a phone call. Wait here."

He got Lapointe on the line again.

"Has the cleaning woman left?"

"I think I can hear her getting ready."

"Can I speak to her?"

He had to wait some time before a woman's voice said, unpleasantly:

"What do you want now?"

"To ask you a question, Madame Bodin. How long have you been living in the Fourteenth Arrondissement?"

"I don't see what that's got to do with it. . . ."

79

"I can easily find out at the police station, where you must be registered."

"Three years."

"And where did you live before?"

"Rue Servan, in the Twelfth."

"Were you ever ill there?"

"My illnesses haven't got anything to do with anybody."

"But you went to Doctor Pardon?"

"He's a good man; he never asks people any questions; he just cures them."

So a little mystery that had been worrying the Superintendent ever since he heard Pardon's story had been cleared up.

"Is that all? Can I do my shopping?"

"Just one more thing . . . You liked Doctor Pardon. . . . So you probably sent acquaintances to him?"

"I may have."

"Try to remember . . . Did you mention him to anyone in the house where you work at present?"

There was a fairly long pause, and Maigret could hear the old woman breathing.

"I don't know."

"To Madame Nahour?"

"She was never ill."

"To Monsieur Oueni? To the maid?"

"I've just told you I don't know! If I can't go and do my shopping, why don't you arrest me?"

Maigret hung up. His pipe had gone out, and he told Janvier to call Orly while he filled another.

"Ask them if the plane that arrived soon after eleven was an Air France or a Swissair flight."

Janvier repeated the question.

"Swissair? Just a minute . . ."

"Tell him to connect you with the office that registers the passengers when they arrive."

"Hello . . . Can you . . ."

A few minutes later Maigret was sure about another point. Pierre Nahour had indeed arrived that morning from Geneva on a Metropolitan, in which he'd got a seat at the last minute.

"Now, chief?"

"As you see, I'm checking. . . . Do you know what time Nahour had dinner last night?"

"At about half past eight . . . He left shortly after half past nine. . . . He ate lamb and then a cake with almonds and raisins."

"Go next door and tell Doctor Collinet, who needs to know before he can tell what time he died. . . ."

Maigret looked up Maître Leroy-Beaulieu's telephone number, and the name seemed familiar to him. When he was on the line, the lawyer exclaimed:

"What is it this time, my dear Superintendent? I haven't had the pleasure of seeing you or speaking to you for some time."

And since Maigret was searching his memory, the lawyer went on:

"The Montrond case, you remember? . . . That old client of mine whose wife . . ."

"Yes . . . yes . . ."

"What can I do for you?"

"I believe the will of a certain Felix Nahour is in your hands."

"Yes, indeed . . . He canceled the old one and made a new one about two years ago."

Do you know why he changed his mind?"

81

There was an embarrassed silence.

"It's an awkward question and I'm in a difficult position. . . . Monsieur Nahour never confided in me. . . . As far as the will is concerned, you realize that I'm bound by professional secrecy. . . . If it's of any use, I can tell you that the reasons were purely personal."

"Felix Nahour was murdered last night in his study."

"Ah! The newspapers haven't mentioned it."

"They will in their next editions."

"Has the murderer been arrested?"

"So far we can only make some contradictory suppositions. Doesn't it happen fairly frequently—and I assume you can tell me this—that when a husband makes his will, his wife makes hers at the same time?"

"I have known this to happen."

"Did it in the case of Monsieur and Madame Nahour?"

"I've never seen Madame Nahour and I haven't had any dealings with her. She's a former beauty queen, isn't she?"

"Exactly."

"When is the funeral taking place?"

"I don't know, because the body is still with the Medical Examiner."

"We usually wait for the funeral before getting in touch with the people concerned. Do you think it will take long?"

"Possibly."

"Have you informed the family?"

"The brother, Pierre Nahour, arrived in Paris this morning. And the father, who was still in Beirut at twelve, must have taken the first flight."

82

"How about Madame Nahour?"

"We're expecting her tomorrow morning."

"Look, my dear Superintendent, I shall send out notice of the meeting this evening. Shall we say for tomorrow afternoon?"

"That would suit me."

"I would like to help you as much as I can, without transgressing our professional rules. All I can tell you is that Madame Nahour, if she knew about the first will, is going to be disagreeably surprised by the second. Is that any use to you?"

"Very much so. Thank you."

Janvier was back in Maigret's office.

"There's something new," murmured Maigret ambiguously. "If I'm right in my thinking, Madame Nahour was the main beneficiary of the first will. About two years ago the husband drew up a second one, and I'd be surprised if he leaves his wife more than the legal minimum."

"Do you think she . . ."

"You forget that I never believe anything before the investigation is over."

He added with a skeptical smile:

"And even then!"

It was decidedly an afterrnoon of telephone calls.

"Get me the Pension des Palmiers at Mougins."

He felt in his pockets and pulled out a piece of paper on which he'd noted the nurse's name.

"See if Mademoiselle Jobe is there."

He went to stand by the window, because he felt numb after having sat so long in his chair. The snowflakes were thinning out. The streets had been lit for some time, and in some places they had been lit all day. There was a traffic jam on Pont Saint-Michel, and three policemen in uniform were trying to sort out the cars and buses with loud blows on their whistles.

"Hello . . . Is that Mademoiselle Jobe? . . . Just a minute, please . . . I'm connecting you with Superintendent Maigret. . . . No . . . From the Police Judiciaire in Paris."

Maigret grabbed the receiver and remained standing, one leg slung over the corner of the desk.

"Hello, Mademoiselle Jobe . . . I suppose the two children are with you? . . . What? . . . You haven't been able to go out because of the rain and the cold? . . . Well, the snow has almost stopped traffic in Paris.

"Have you heard from Monsieur Nahour? . . . He telephoned you yesterday? . . . At about what time? . . . Ten in the morning . . . Yes, I see. . . . He used to call before your walk or in the evening. . . . Did he have any special reason for calling you? . . . None in particular. . . He did it two or three times a week. . . .

"And Madame Nahour? . . . Less often? . . . Once? . . . Anything up to two weeks between one call and another? . . .

"No, Mademoiselle . . . I'm asking you these questions because Monsieur Nahour was murdered last night. . . . Nobody's been arrested. . . . May I ask you how long you've been working for this family? . . . For five years? . . . Since the first child was born.

"Unfortunately, I can't come to Mougins right now. . . . I may have to send instructions to the Police Judiciaire in Cannes so that they can take down your state-

84

ment. . . . No, of course not. . . . Don't worry . . . I understand your position perfectly.

"Look, when you entered their service the Nahours traveled a great deal, didn't they? . . . Yes . . . To Cannes, Deauville, Evian . . . Most of the time they rented a villa for the season, or for part of the season. . . . Did you go with them? . . . Frequently? . . . Yes . . . I can hear you. . . .

"You lived in the Ritz with them and the little girl. . . . Then, three years later, the boy was born. . . . That's what happened, isn't it? . . . He isn't a sickly child who needs a warmer climate than Paris's, is he? . . . If I'm not mistaken, he's two years old now. . . . And a real little devil . . .

"By all means . . . go ahead . . . I'll stay on the line. . . ."

He nodded to Janvier:

"The children are quarreling in the next room. . . . She seems a very nice girl. Her answers are clear and she makes them without hesitating. Long may it last! . . . Hello . . . Yes . . . So Monsieur Nahour paid more attention to his children than his wife did. . . . You sent him a short report on their health and what they did every day. . . .

"Did you notice any tension between husband and wife? . . . Hard to tell, I know. . . . They each led a life of their own. . . . That didn't surprise you? . . . Only to start with? . . . You got used to it. . . .

"Did they come and see them together? . . . Hardly ever? . . . I greatly appreciate your assistance. . . . I quite understand that you don't know anything else. . . . Thank you."

85

Maigret gave a deep sigh and lit his pipe, which had gone out.

"And now comes the worst part. . . . I say that out of habit, really, because Cayotte is very agreeable as magistrates go."

He took Pardon's report off his desk and walked slowly toward the examining magistrates' offices in the Palais de Justice. Cayotte had not been given a modern office, and his room was straight out of a nineteenth-century novel.

Even the clerk seemed out of a drawing by Forain or Steinlen, and he all but wore sleeve covers.

Since there was no room on the black wooden shelves, files were accumulating on the floor, and the lamp hanging over the Magistrate's desk had lost its shade.

"Sit down, Maigret . . . Well? . . ."

The Superintendent did not try to hold back. For more than an hour he remained seated on a rickety chair, telling all he knew. When he finally left, the smoke from his pipe and the cigarettes the Magistrate chain-smoked formed a thick mist around the light bulb.

Maigret was at the airport at half past nine in the morning, although the plane from Amsterdam was not expected until 9:57. It was Sunday. While he was shaving, Maigret had heard radio warnings to motorists not to drive except when absolutely necessary because the snow crust on the roads had become harder and slipperier than ever.

Lucas had driven him and was waiting for him in the Police Judiciaire car. There was more bustle at the airport than in all the streets of Paris, and the air was hot, an almost human heat, which sent the blood to one's head.

After drinking a glass of beer at one of the bars, the Superintendent felt himself growing crimson in the face and regretted having put on the stifling scarf Madame Maigret had knitted for him and that she insisted he wear.

The loudspeakers announced a delay of about ten minutes for the flight from Copenhagen via Amsterdam, and he strolled around looking at the passport officials, who glanced briefly at every traveler and stamped or did not stamp the passports accordingly.

The day before, at about eight o'clock, Keulemans had telephoned him at Boulevard Richard-Lenoir just as he was sitting down to dinner after turning on the television.

"Lina Nahour has booked two seats on the flight leaving for Orly at 8:45."

"Is Alvaredo going with her?"

"No. The second seat is for her friend Anna Keegel. The young man booked a seat on the flight leaving at 11:22 and arriving in Paris at 12:45."

"Did they telephone each other again?"

"At about five o'clock. Lina Nahour simply said what time she was leaving and added that her friend was going with her. He said he'd take the next plane. When he asked her how she was, she said she felt much better and her temperature had dropped to 99.5."

The flight's arrival was announced, and Maigret stuck his face to the cold window, gazing at the people moving around the aircraft.

He did not recognize the young woman among the

passengers, including four children, who were the first to disembark, and he started to think that she had changed her mind when he saw a young woman dressed in a seal coat leaning on her companion's arm as she disembarked.

Anna Keegel, who was small and dark, was wearing a thick bright-green wool coat.

At the last moment, the hostess helped Lina get into the little bus where the other passengers were already standing, and the doors closed.

Having been the last to leave the plane, the two women were the last to have their passports examined, and Maigret, leaning against the barrier, had plenty of time to look at them.

Was Lina Nahour really beautiful? It was a question of taste. She had a light and fresh Nordic complexion, as Pardon had said, a small pointed nose, and pale-blue eyes.

That morning her features were strained and she seemed to have considerable difficulty standing up.

Anna Keegel was ugly in a pleasant way, and even though this was no time for laughter, one felt that she had a sense of humor.

He followed them at a distance to customs, where they waited a few minutes for a green suitcase and another, cheaper-looking, case, which must belong to Anna.

A porter took their luggage and hailed a taxi outside the terminal, while Maigret got into the police car next to Lucas.

"Is that them?"

"Yes. Don't let them give you the slip."

It wasn't difficult, because the taxi driver drove carefully and they took three-quarters of an hour to get to Avenue du Parc-Montsouris.

"Did you think they'd go somewhere else?"

"I didn't think anything. I just wanted to make sure. Park behind the taxi when it stops and wait for me."

The two women got out and, before going through the garden gate, Lina Nahour looked the house up and down, seemed to hesitate, and finally let her friend lead her in.

Maigret overtook them and arrived at the front door before them.

"Who are you?" asked Lina, frowning.

She had a slight accent.

"Superintendent Maigret. I'm investigating your husband's death. May I follow you in?"

Although she didn't protest, she looked uneasy and pulled her coat around her. The taxi driver carried the cases to the front door, and it was Anna Keegel who opened her bag to pay the fare.

Fat Torrence, who was on day duty, opened the door without saying a word, and Lina looked at him with amazement rather than anxiety.

She seemed not to know what to do or where to go; she hesitated to go up to her room or into the study.

"Where's the body?" she asked Maigret.

"At the Medico-Legal Institute."

Was she relieved that it was no longer in the house? She seemed to shiver, but she was so tense that her movements were really reflexes.

She finally reached for the door handle of the study, but just as she was about to turn it, the door was opened

89

from the inside and Pierre Nahour appeared, surprised to find four people in the hall.

"Hello, Pierre . . ." she said, giving him her hand.

Did the banker from Geneva really hesitate? At all events, he held out his hand, too.

"Where did it happen?"

Pierre Nahour stood back to let Lina, her friend, and the Superintendent in, while Torrence stayed in the hall.

"Here . . . behind the desk."

She hesitantly went a few steps, saw the patch of blood, and turned away.

"How did it happen?"

"Someone shot him."

"Did he die at once?"

Pierre Nahour remained calm, fairly cold, and watched his sister-in-law with no visible feeling on his face.

"We don't know. . . . The cleaning woman found him when she came to work in the morning."

Seeing her so unsteady, her friend led her to an armchair, in which she sat down cautiously; her back must have been hurting. She showed that she wanted a cigarette, and Anna Keegel lit one and handed it to her.

The silence was rather embarrassing. Even Maigret felt slightly awkward in view of the physical, and probably also the mental, condition of the young woman, whose nerves must have been strained to breaking point.

"Do you know if he suffered?"

"We don't know," said Pierre Nahour dryly.

"At what time did it . . . did it happen?"

"Probably between midnight and one o'clock."

"Wasn't anyone in the house?"

"Fouad was at the club and Nelly was asleep. . . . She says she didn't hear a thing."

"Do I have to go to a meeting at the lawyer's?"

"He called me, yes. . . . Tomorrow afternoon . . . My father arrived last night and is resting in his room at the Hotel Raspail."

"What shall I do?" she asked, talking to no one in particular.

After a silence still more unpleasant than the previous ones, it was her friend who replied, in Dutch.

"Do you think . . .?" she asked her in French. "Yes, maybe that's the best thing. . . . I wouldn't have the courage to sleep in this house."

She looked around for Maigret.

"I'm going to a hotel with my friend and my maid."

She didn't even ask his permission, as a suspect would have, but simply announced her decision.

Then she turned to her brother-in-law again:

"Is Nelly upstairs? Where's Madame Bodin?"

"She hasn't come. Nelly's in her room."

"I'm going up to get some clothes. . . . Will you come and help me, Anna?"

When they were alone together, the two men looked at each other in silence.

"How did your father take it, Monsieur Nahour?"

"Pretty badly . . . My sister came with him, and they've both gone to rest in the hotel. . . . I insisted that they shouldn't stay here."

"Are you staying?"

"I'd rather. . . . Are you starting to get an idea who the murderer could be, Monsieur Maigret?"

"How about you?"

91

"I don't know. . . . Why didn't you question my sister-in-law?"

"I'm waiting for her to settle down in a hotel. For the moment, she obviously couldn't bear it."

They were standing up, and Pierre Nahour had a hard look on his face.

"I would like to ask you a question," said the Superintendent gently. "You've read your brother's letters and you've had a chance to talk to Oueni. . . . He doesn't seem prepared to co-operate with us. Maybe, with you . . ."

"I tried to get something out of him yesterday evening, but without much success."

"The number of possible suspects seems fairly limited, on one condition. . . ."

"Which one?"

"Suppose that your brother, contrary to what you first thought, gambled not only for himself recently, but also for a group, as he has been known to do in the past."

"I see what you're driving at, Superintendent, but you are quite wrong. My brother was an honest man, like all the Nahours. He was scrupulous to the point of fussiness, as I realized when I was reading his letters. . . .

"It is out of the question that he would have cheated a group of a single penny, and that he was murdered for vengeance."

"I'm glad to hear you say that. . . . I'm sorry that my job forces me to take every possibility into account. . . . It may be Oueni's presence in the house that put that idea into my head."

"I don't understand."

"Don't you think Oueni's position is rather equivocal? . . . He's neither a secretary nor a manservant or chauffeur, and he's not an equal, either. . . . Hence the possibility that he was watching your brother, representing a group."

Nahour smiled ironically.

"If anyone else were to say that to me I'd say he'd been reading too many thrillers. . . . I mentioned the sense of family feeling in Lebanon. Well, the family doesn't stop at one's relatives. It sometimes includes old retainers, and friends can sometimes live in the house and be treated as equals."

"Would you have chosen Oueni?"

"No . . . First, because I don't like the man, and then, because I married young and my wife's enough for me. . . . Don't forget that Felix remained a bachelor until he was thirty-five. In the family we were all sure that he'd never marry."

"Just a minute, please . . ."

Maigret, who had heard some steps on the stairs, went to open the door. Lina had changed her dress and was now wearing her mink coat. Nelly Velthuis followed her, a distant look in her eyes, carrying a case, and Anna Keegel, carrying more luggage, brought up the rear.

"Could you get me a taxi, Pierre? . . . I shouldn't have let mine go."

She looked at the Superintendent questioningly, and Maigret asked:

"Which hotel are you going to? . . . The Ritz?"

"Oh no! That brings back too many memories. . . .

93

Wait a minute . . . what's the name of that hotel on the corner of Rue de Rivoli, near the Place Vendôme?"

"The Hotel du Louvre?"

"That's right. . . . We'll go to the Hotel du Louvre."

"I'll call on you later, because I shall have to ask you a few questions."

"The taxi's on its way."

It was almost twelve. It was Janvier's turn to go to Orly, wait for Alvaredo, and follow him.

"Good-bye, Pierre . . . What time is the meeting tomorrow, and who's the lawyer?"

"Three o'clock, Maître Leroy-Beaulieu, on Boulevard Saint-Germain."

"No need to write it down," interrupted Maigret, "I'll give you the address at the hotel."

It took some time to get the luggage and the three passengers into the car. Lina was obviously shivering on the sidewalk and looked around as though she did not recognize a setting that was familiar to her.

Pierre Nahour shut the door, and Maigret thought he saw a curtain move at a window that must have been Oueni's.

He said to Lucas as he got in next to him:

"Follow them . . . They're going to the Hotel du Louvre, but I'd rather be certain. . . . So far I'm not sure that I've heard one word of truth in this whole case."

The streets were as empty as they were in August, without the buses full of tourists. The taxi stopped in front of the Hotel du Louvre. Lina and her friend went in first, probably to see whether there were any free rooms. A few seconds later a porter came for their luggage while the maid looked at the meter and paid the fare.

"Go and park the car somewhere and meet me at the bar. I must give her time to get to her room and make herself comfortable."

Besides, he was thirsty.

❧ 5 ❧

THE BAR WAS DARK AND SILENT. TWO ENGLISHMEN SITTING
on tall stools were moving their lips, but one couldn't
hear what they were saying. The walls were covered
with oak panels, and the lamps in sconces gave out a
dim light only every four or five yards. In a corner a
young woman sat waiting, in front of a pinkish cocktail.
In the opposite corner four men occasionally leaned
toward each other.

Here, too, it was Sunday, a hollow day, outside reality. Through the cream-colored curtains one could just
see a little dirty snow, black trees, and the head of a
passer-by.

"Check your coat, sir?"

"I'm sorry. . . ."

His investigations usually led him to local bistros or
noisy bars near the Champs-Elysées, and not to palaces.
He took off his coat and sighed with relief as he pulled
off his hot scarf.

"A beer," he ordered under his breath to the barman,

who looked at him as though he were trying to remember where he had seen him before.

"Carlsberg . . . Heineken?"

"Either."

Good old Lucas was also stopped by the young lady in the checkroom.

"What will you have?"

"How about you, chief?"

"I ordered a beer."

"The same for me, then."

The word GRILLROOM was written in weakly lit letters over an open door, through which came a faint noise of plates.

"Are you hungry?"

"Not very."

"Do you know the room numbers?"

"437, 438, and 439. Two bedrooms and a small sitting room."

"How about Nelly?"

"She sleeps in one of the rooms. 437 is a large room with two beds, for Madame Nahour and her friend."

"I'll be back at once."

In the vast marble hallway Maigret walked toward a door marked TELEPHONE.

"Can you give me room 437, please?"

"Just a minute . . ."

"Hello . . . Madame Nahour?"

"Who's speaking?"

"Superintendent Maigret."

"This is Anna Keegel speaking. Madame Nahour is in the bath."

"Ask her if she'd rather I came up in about ten

minutes or whether she wants to have lunch first."

He waited for some time. He could hear indistinct voices.

"Hello . . . She isn't hungry, because she ate on the plane, but she'd rather you didn't come up in less than half an hour."

Maigret and Lucas went into the grillroom a few minutes later. It was as well upholstered as the bar, with the same wooden panels, the same sconces, and small lights on the tables. Only three or four of the tables were taken, and everybody was whispering, as if in church. The maître d'hôtel, the chefs, and the waiters came and went in silence, like the priests of some cult.

When he was handed an enormous menu, Maigret shook his head.

"*Assiette anglaise,*" he muttered.

"For me, too."

"Two cold meats," corrected the maître d'hôtel.

"And a beer."

"I'll send you the wine steward."

"Can you telephone the Quai and tell them we're here? Tell them to try to get in touch with Janvier, who must still be at Orly. Give them the room number."

Maigret suddenly looked heavy, and Lucas, who recognized this symptom, took care not to ask him any unnecessary questions.

The meal was eaten in almost complete silence, under the blasé eyes of the maître d'hôtel and the waiters.

"Will you have some coffee?"

A man in Turkish costume served them with affected gestures.

"You'd better come up with me."

They got to the fourth floor and knocked on door number 437, but it was 438 that opened.

"This way . . ." said Anna Keegel.

She must also have had a bath, or a shower, because she had a lock of damp hair.

"Come in . . . I'll tell Lina."

In the small sitting room everything was soft and understated, the pale-gray walls, the light-blue armchairs, the table painted ivory white. Somebody could be heard moving about in the room on the left, probably Nelly Velthuis still unpacking.

They waited for some time, standing, ill at ease, and finally the two women came in. Maigret was surprised, because he expected Lina Nahour to be in bed.

She had just combed her hair and was wearing no make-up. She had on a faded pink velvet bathrobe.

She looked frail and vulnerable. If she was making an effort, it was not visible, and the tension of the morning had disappeared.

She was astonished to see two men instead of one and she looked at Lucas interrogatively.

"One of my detectives," explained Maigret.

"Sit down, gentlemen."

She sat down on the sofa, and her friend came and sat next to her.

"I'm sorry to bother you so soon after your arrival, but you do understand that I have some questions to ask, don't you?"

She lit a cigarette, and the fingers holding the match trembled slightly.

"You may smoke."

"Thank you."

He did not fill his pipe immediately.

"May I ask where you were on Friday night?"

"At what time?"

"I would like you to tell me all you did that evening and that night."

"I left the house at about eight o'clock."

"At about the same time as your husband, you mean?"

"I don't know where he was just then."

"Did you usually go out without telling him where you were going?"

"We were both free to go where we liked."

"Did you take your car?"

"No. The roads were icy, and I didn't want to drive."

"Did you call a taxi?"

"Yes."

"From the telephone in your room?"

"Yes. Of course."

She talked like a little girl reciting her lesson, and her innocent eyes reminded the Superintendent of somebody. It was only after several sentences that he thought of the maid, her almost transparent pupils, her childish expression.

He found that Lina behaved in the same way, almost as though one of the two women were copying the other, so similar were their expressions and even the movement of their eyelids.

"Where did you go?"

"To a large restaurant on the Champs-Elysées. The Marignan."

She had hesitated before saying this last word.

"Do you frequently have dinner at the Marignan?"

"Sometimes."

"Alone?"

"Usually."

"Where were you sitting?"

"In the main room."

Where there were usually about a hundred customers, so it was impossible to check her alibi.

"Did anyone join you?"

"No."

"Did you have an appointment?"

"I remained alone until the end of the meal."

"What time was that?"

"I don't know. Maybe ten o'clock."

"Did you pass through the bar first?"

Another pause, and then she shook her head.

Now the more nervous of the two of them was her friend, Anna Keegel, who looked at Lina and the Superintendent in turn, moving her head at each question.

"Then?"

"I walked along the Champs-Elysées to get some air."

"In spite of the slippery sidewalks?"

"The sidewalks had been cleared. When I was almost opposite the Lido I took a taxi and went back home."

"You still hadn't seen your husband, who was back around ten?"

"I didn't see him. I went up to my room, where Nelly had just finished packing my suitcase."

"Because you'd decided to go on a trip?"

With complete candor, she replied:

"I'd decided the week before."

"What was your destination?"

"Why . . . Amsterdam, of course."

She started talking to Anna Keegel in Dutch. Anna got up, went into the bedroom, and came back a little later with a letter. It was dated January 6, and was not written in French or English.

"You can have it translated. I'm telling Anna to expect me on January 15."

"Had you booked a seat on the plane?"

"No. I had first wanted to go by train. There is a train at 11:12."

"Were you going to take your maid?"

"There's no room for her in Anna's apartment."

Although Maigret wanted her to swallow the hook completely, he felt a certain admiration for the calm way in which she lied.

"Did you stop on the ground floor on your way out?"

"No. The taxi Nelly had called was already outside the door."

"Did you say good-bye to your husband?"

"No. He knew."

"Did you drive to the Gare du Nord?"

"We arrived late because of the bad street conditions. Since the train had left, I went to Orly."

"Passing by Boulevard Voltaire?"

She didn't blink. It was Anna Keegel who winced.

"Where's that?"

"I'm sorry to have to tell you that you know as well as I do. How did you get Doctor Pardon's address?"

There was a long silence. She lit another cigarette, stood up, walked a few steps, and sat down again. If she was upset, it was not visible. She seemed to be thinking what she should say.

"What do you know?" she asked Maigret in her turn, looking him straight in the eye.

"That you were wounded by your husband in the study by a bullet from a 6.35 with a mother-of-pearl handle, which used to belong to you and which he kept in a drawer of his desk."

With her elbow on the arm of the chair, she held her chin in her hand and gazed at the Superintendent with curiosity. She was like a model schoolgirl listening to her teacher.

"You did not leave the house in a taxi but in the red car of a friend named Vicente Alvaredo. He took you to Boulevard Voltaire, where he told an incredible story about an attack by an unknown motorist. . . .

"Doctor Pardon, to whom you didn't say a word, put a temporary dressing on the wound. You returned to his waiting room and, as he was taking off his coat and washing his hands, you left without a sound. . . . "

"What do you want out of me?"

She was not disconcerted. One could have sworn that she was smiling at him, just like a little girl who has been caught out and who considers a lie only a big sin.

"I want the truth."

"I'd rather you asked me questions."

That was clever, too, because it meant she could find out exactly what the police knew. Nevertheless, Maigret joined in.

"Was this letter really written on January 6? Before you answer, let me tell you that we can check that by analyzing the ink."

"It was written on January 6."

"Did your husband know?"

"He must have."

"Know what?"

"That I was going to leave soon."

"Why?"

"Because life had been unbearable for some time."

"How long?"

"Months."

"Two years?"

"Perhaps."

"Ever since you met Vicente Alvaredo?"

Anna Keegel was getting increasingly nervous, and her foot touched Lina's pink slipper as if by chance.

"That's about right."

"Did your husband know about your affair?"

"I don't know. Somebody may have seen Vicente and me. We didn't hide."

"Do you think it normal for a married woman . . ."

"Only just!"

"What do you mean?"

"Felix and I had been living like strangers for years."

"And yet you had a second child two years ago."

"Because my husband wanted a son. It's just as well it wasn't another girl."

"Is your son by him?"

"Definitely. When I met Alvaredo I'd only just got over my confinement and I was beginning to go out."

"Have you had any other lovers?"

"Believe it or not, he was the first."

"What were your plans for the evening of the fourteenth?"

"I don't understand?"

"On the sixth you wrote to your friend that you were arriving in Amsterdam on the fifteenth."

Anna Keegel started speaking to her in Dutch, but Lina, sure of herself, shook her head and continued to

104

look at the Superintendent with the same assurance.

Maigret had at last lit his pipe.

"I'll try to explain. Alvaredo wanted me to get a divorce and marry him. I asked him for a week, because I knew it wouldn't be easy. There never has been a divorce in the Nahour family, and Felix wanted to keep up appearances.

"We decided that I'd talk to him about it on the fourteenth and that whatever he said we would leave for Amsterdam immediately."

"Why Amsterdam?"

She seemed surprised that the Superintendent did not understand.

"Because that's where I spent most of my childhood and my youth. Vicente didn't know Holland. I wanted to show it to him. Once the divorce was obtained, we were going to see his parents in Colombia before getting married."

"Have you money of your own?"

"No, of course not. But we didn't need the Nahours' money."

She added with a slightly naïve pride:

"The Alvaredos are richer than they are and they own most of the gold mines in Colombia."

"Good. So you left at about eight without saying anything to your husband. Alvaredo was waiting for you in his Alfa Romeo. Where did you dine?"

"In a little restaurant on Boulevard du Montparnasse where Vicente eats nearly all his meals, since he lives next door."

"Were you worried about your husband's possible reaction when he knew about your decision?"

"No."

"Why, since he was against divorce?"

"Because he had no way of keeping me."

"Did he still love you?"

"I'm not sure he ever loved me."

"Why would he have married you?"

"Maybe to be seen around with a pretty, well-dressed woman. It was at Deauville, the year I was chosen Miss Europe. We met several times in the rooms and hallways of the casino. One evening I found him next to me at a roulette table. He pushed some large rectangular chips toward me and whispered:

" 'Play on fourteen.' "

"Did fourteen come up?"

"Not the first time, but the third. It came up twice, consecutively, and I'd never seen as much money as when I cashed in my chips that evening at the bank."

The tables had turned. This time it was her own story that seemed the most plausible, almost obvious.

"He found out the number of my room and he sent me flowers. We dined together several times. He seemed very shy. I felt he wasn't used to talking to women."

"And yet he was thirty-five years old."

"I'm not so sure he had known any other woman before me. Then he took me to Biarritz."

"Without ever asking you for anything?"

"In Biarritz, where he spent most of his nights in the casino, as he had in Deauville, he came to my room at about five o'clock one morning. He usually didn't drink. But that night I could smell alcohol on his breath."

"Was he drunk?"

"He'd drunk a glass or two to summon up courage."

"Is that when it happened?"

"Yes. He didn't stay more than half an hour with me. And in the five months that followed he didn't come to see me more than ten times. Nevertheless, he asked me to marry him. I accepted."

"Because he was rich?"

"Because I liked the life he led, from one hotel to the next, from one casino to the next. We got married in Cannes, but we continued to have separate rooms. He wanted it. He was very modest. I think he was rather ashamed of being so fat, because at that period he was fatter than he was in the last few years."

"Was he tender with you?"

"He treated me like a little girl. He didn't change any of his habits, and we were accompanied everywhere by Oueni, with whom he spent more time than with me."

"How did you get on with Oueni?"

"I don't like him."

"Why?"

"I don't know. Perhaps because he had too much influence over my husband. And perhaps because he belongs to another race, one I don't understand."

"What was Oueni's attitude toward you?"

"He appeared not to see me. He must despise me profoundly, since he despises all women. One day, when I was bored, I asked to be allowed to have a Dutch girl as a maid. I put an advertisement in the papers in Amsterdam and I chose Nelly because she seemed cheerful."

She was smiling now, while her friend, who looked

worried, seemed not to approve of the turn the conversation had taken.

"Let's get back to Friday evening. What time did you get back to the house?"

"At about half past eleven."

"Did you and Alvaredo stay in the restaurant until then?"

"No. We went to his apartment to get his suitcase. I helped him pack it. We chatted and had a drink."

"Once he was at your home, did he stay in the car?"

"Yes."

"You went into the study?"

"No. I went up to my room and changed. I asked Nelly if Felix was downstairs, and she answered that she'd heard him come back."

"Did she also tell you if he was alone or with his 'secretary'?"

"With his secretary."

"Didn't that upset you in view of the conversation you expected to have?"

"I was used to seeing Oueni there with him. I don't know what the time was when I went down. I'd already put my coat on. Nelly followed me with the suitcase, which she left in the hall, and we kissed each other."

"Was she going to join you?"

"As soon as I told her to."

"Did she go up to her room? Without waiting for the result of your encounter?"

"She knew I'd made up my mind and nothing would change it."

The telephone rang on the little round table. Maigret signaled to Lucas to answer.

"Hello . . . Yes . . . He's here. . . . Here he is."

Maigret knew that he would hear Janvier's voice.

"He's arrived, chief. He's home, on Boulevard . . ."

"Boulevard du Montparnasse."

"Did you know that already? He lives in a furnished studio. I'm in a little bar opposite the building."

"Stay there . . . I'll see you later."

And Lina, looking as natural as ever, asked, as if it were self-evident:

"Has Vicente arrived?"

"Yes. He's at his apartment."

"Why are the police watching him?"

"It's their duty to watch all suspects."

"Why should he even be a suspect? He's never set foot in the house on Avenue du Parc-Montsouris."

"That's what you say."

"Don't you believe me?"

"I never know when you're lying or telling the truth. By the way, how did you get Doctor Pardon's address?"

"Nelly gave it to me. She was told by our cleaning woman, who had lived in the district. I had to have medical aid immediately, as far from the house as possible. . . ."

"Very well!" he muttered, without conviction, because he was no longer prepared to believe anything. "You kissed Nelly Velthuis in the hall, where your suitcase was. She went upstairs and you went into the study. You found your husband there working with Oueni."

She nodded.

"Did you mention your departure right away?"

"Yes. I told him I was going to Amsterdam, from

109

where my lawyer would write him a letter and make arrangements for a divorce."

"How did he take that?"

"He looked at me for a long time in silence, and then murmured:

" 'It's not possible.' "

"Did it occur to him to send Oueni out?"

"No."

"Was Nahour sitting at his desk?"

"Yes."

"Was Oueni sitting opposite him?"

"No. Oueni was standing by his side, holding some papers. I can't remember my exact words. I was a little nervous in spite of it all."

"Did Alvaredo advise you to carry a gun? Did he give you one?"

"I didn't have a gun. What use would it have been? I told him my decision was final, that nothing would change my mind, and I started to walk toward the door. It was then that I heard an explosion and felt a pain, like a burn, in my shoulder.

"I must have turned around, because I can remember Felix standing there holding a pistol. Above all, I can remember his eyes, wide open, as though he had just realized what he had done."

"What about Oueni?"

"He was standing next to him, motionless."

"What did you do?"

"I was afraid I was going to faint. I didn't want that to happen in the house, where I would have been at the mercy of the two men. I rushed to the door and found myself standing by the car door which Vicente opened for me."

"Did you hear a second explosion?"

"No. I told Vicente to drive me to Boulevard Voltaire, to a doctor I knew. . . ."

"But you didn't know Doctor Pardon."

"I didn't have time to explain. I felt very ill."

"Why didn't you go to Alvaredo's apartment, which was almost next door, and why didn't he call his own doctor?"

"Because I didn't want to cause a scandal. I was in a hurry to be in Amsterdam and I was sure the police wouldn't find out. That was why I didn't say anything at the doctor's, in case he should recognize my accent.

"I didn't expect him to ask any questions. I didn't know the bullet had stayed in the wound and I didn't know how deep it was. I just wanted to stop the blood."

"What means of transport did you and Vicente expect to take to Amsterdam?"

"His car. When I left the doctor, I felt too weak to spend hours in a car, and Vicente took me in a taxi straight to Anna's flat, and I told him to go to a hotel, where he was to wait until I felt better. We were going to have separate rooms until the divorce."

"To avoid being sued on grounds of adultery?"

"Precautions were no longer necessary. Felix couldn't refuse a divorce after the shot."

"So, if I'm right in my thinking, it was to your advantage."

She looked at him and couldn't help smiling maliciously.

"Yes," she admitted.

The strangest thing of all was that it seemed quite likely, and Maigret wanted to believe her, so frankly

111

did she appear to answer his questions. As he watched her face, which had remained as childlike as Nelly Velthuis', Maigret could understand Nahour treating her like a little girl, and he could understand Vicente Alvaredo falling sufficiently in love with her to want to marry her despite her husband and her two children.

It was warm in the comfortable, plush sitting room and it was easy to be almost engulfed by it. Lucas himself looked like a large cat purring.

"I would like to add one more point, Madame Nahour: there is nobody to confirm your statements. According to you, there were three of you in the study when the first shot was fired."

"You have Fouad as a witness."

"Unfortunately for you, he pretends that he returned to the house only after one in the morning, and it has been established that he left the club on Boulevard Saint-Michel at about the same time."

"He's lying."

"He was seen there."

"What if he went there after the shot?"

"We'll try to check that."

"You can question Nelly, too."

"She can't speak French, can she?"

He felt her hesitate, and she answered indirectly:

"She can speak English."

Suddenly Maigret's massive body seemed to unfold itself. Without a sound he crept up to the door of the adjoining room and opened it suddenly. The maid nearly fell into his arms and had great difficulty keeping her balance.

"Have you been listening long?"

On the verge of tears, she shook her head. She had changed her suit for a black satin dress and a white apron with embroidered scallops, and she wore a cap on her head.

"Did you understand what we said?"

She said yes, and then no, looking at her mistress for help.

"She understands a little French," said Lina. "But whenever she tries to talk, particularly to the local shopkeepers, they make fun of her."

"Come here, Nelly. Don't stay glued to the door. How long have you known that Madame Nahour was leaving for Amsterdam on Friday evening?"

"One week."

"You're not talking to her, but to me."

She turned to the Superintendent reluctantly, still hesitating to look him in the face.

"At what time did you pack the suitcase?"

She was obviously translating the answer in her mind.

"Eight o'clock."

"Why did you lie when I questioned you yesterday?"

"I don't know. . . . I was frightened."

"What of?"

"I don't know."

"Did someone in the house frighten you?"

She shook her head violently, and her cap went askew.

"Did you see Madame Nahour again at about ten?"

"Yes."

"Where?"

"In room."

"Who brought down the suitcase?"

"I."

"Where did your mistress go?"

"Study."

"Did you hear a shot later?"

"Yes."

"One or two shots?"

She looked toward Lina again and replied:

"One."

"Did you come down?"

"No."

"Why not?"

She shrugged her shoulders, as if to say she didn't know. It was not a case of one of the two women copying the other. Each one had taken certain characteristics from the other, so that the maid was now rather like a muddled answer from Lina.

"Did you hear Oueni go to his room?"

"No."

"Did you go to sleep at once?"

"Yes."

"Did you try to find out who was wounded or dead?"

"Saw Madame from window. Heard door and saw Madame and car."

"Thank you. All I hope is that when your statement is recorded tomorrow you don't give us a third version of the facts."

The sentence was obviously too long and too difficult for her, and Madame Nahour translated it into Dutch while the girl turned very red and hurried away.

"What I've just said goes for you, too, Madame Nahour. I didn't want you to undergo an official interrogation today. Tomorrow I'll call you and make an appointment. I'll come around in person, or one of

114

my detectives will, to take down your statement."

"There's a third witness," she added.

"Alvaredo. I know. I'll see him when I leave here. Since I don't trust the telephone, Inspector Lucas will stay in your suite until I relieve him."

She didn't protest.

"Can I have some food sent up? My friend Anna is always hungry. She's real Dutch woman. As for me, I'm going to bed."

"May I go into your room a moment?"

The room was fairly untidy; clothes had been thrown hurriedly onto the bed and shoes on the carpet. The telephone was plugged into the wall. Maigret unplugged it, brought it into the sitting room, and then did the same thing to the telephone in Nelly's room.

Nelly, who was putting some clothes away in the drawers, looked at him bitterly, as though he had scolded her.

"I'm sorry about these precautions," he said as he left the two women.

And Lina replied with a smile:

"It's your job, isn't it?"

The doorman called him a taxi. One could now just distinguish a pale sun behind the clouds, and children were sliding on the snow in the Jardins du Luxembourg. Three or four of them had even brought their toboggans.

He found the bistro where Janvier was waiting for him, seated close to the misty window, which he wiped from time to time.

"A beer," he ordered in a tired voice.

The interrogation had exhausted him, and he still felt the clamminess of the little sitting room cling to his body.

"Has he been out?"

"No. I suppose he ate on the plane. He must be waiting for a phone call."

"He'll have a long wait."

Maigret could have had the telephone tapped, like his colleague in Amsterdam, but maybe because he belonged to the old school, or more probably because of the way he was brought up, he hesitated to resort to this procedure unless he was dealing with professionals.

"Lucas stayed at the Hotel du Louvre. Come and see the young man with me. I don't know him yet. By the way, what's he like?"

The beer was refreshing and helped him return to reality. It was good to see a real bar again, with sawdust on the floor and a waiter in a blue apron.

"Very handsome, casually elegant, with a rather distant expression."

"Did he try to see whether he was being followed?"

"Not as far as I could tell."

"Come along."

They crossed the street and went into a prosperous-looking building, where they took the elevator.

"Third floor," said Janvier. "I inquired. He's lived in the studio for three years."

There was no plate or visiting card on the door, which opened a few seconds after Maigret had rung. A very dark young man, rather tall, said, extremely politely:

"Come in, gentlemen . . . I was expecting you. . . . Superintendent Maigret, I presume?"

He did not hold out his hand but led them into a light sitting room with modern furniture and pictures and a balcony window looking onto the street.

"Won't you take your coats off?"

"One question first, Monsieur Alvaredo. Madame Nahour telephoned you yesterday in Amsterdam to say that her husband was dead. She telephoned again that afternoon to tell you which flight she was taking with her friend. You left Amsterdam this morning, and the Dutch papers of last night couldn't have mentioned the case."

Alvaredo turned casually to the sofa and picked up a Paris paper of the day before.

"There's even a photograph of you on the third page," he said with a bantering smile.

The two men took off their overcoats.

"Can I give you a drink?"

A variety of bottles and several glasses stood on a low table. Only one glass was off the tray and still held a little amber-colored liquid.

"Listen to me, Monsieur Alvaredo. Before asking you any further questions I want to tell you that so far in this case I've been constantly confronted with people who take considerable liberties with the truth."

"Do you mean Lina?"

"She and other people whom I do not have to mention to you. First of all, I would like to know when you last set foot in the Nahours' house."

"If you don't mind my saying so, Superintendent, I don't find your trap very subtle. You must already know that I've never been into that house, either on Friday night or at any other time."

"Do you know if Monsieur Nahour knew about your affair with his wife?"

"I don't know, since I've only seen him a couple of times, in the distance, at a gambling table."

"Do you know Fouad?"

"Lina has mentioned him, but I've never met him."

"On Friday evening you did not hide. Instead, you waited in a very obvious car just outside the gate."

"We didn't have to hide any longer, since we'd made up our minds and Lina was going to inform her husband."

"Were you worried about the result of that conversation?"

"Why worried? Lina had decided to leave, and he couldn't keep her by force."

He added rather bitterly:

"We're not in the Near East."

"Did you hear a shot?"

"I heard a muffled sound, which I couldn't place at once. A second later the door opened and Lina rushed out to the sidewalk, dragging her suitcase. I just had time to open the door. She seemed exhausted. And she told me about it as we drove off."

"Did you know Doctor Pardon?"

"I'd never heard of him. She gave me his address."

"Did you still plan to go to Amsterdam by car?"

"I didn't realize how seriously she'd been wounded. She was bleeding profusely. I was very worried."

"Which didn't prevent you from lying to the doctor."

"I thought it better not to tell him the truth."

"And to leave his office without a word . . ."

"So that he wouldn't take down our names."

"Did you know that Nahour kept a weapon in the drawer of his desk?"

"Lina had mentioned it to me."

"Was she frightened of her husband?"

"He wasn't a man one could be frightened of."

"How about Oueni?"

"She didn't say much about him."

"But he played an important part in that house."

"As far as his master was concerned, maybe, but he had nothing to do with Lina."

"Are you sure?"

Suddenly the blood rushed to Alvaredo's cheeks and ears, and he replied between his teeth:

"What are you hinting?"

"I'm not hinting anything, except that Fouad, who influenced Nahour, could influence the fate of Madame Nahour indirectly."

The young man calmed down, embarrassed at having lost his temper.

"You are very passionate, Monsieur Alvaredo."

"I'm in love . . ." he said dryly.

"May I ask how long you've been in Paris?"

"Three and a half years."

"Are you a student?"

"I took a law degree in Bogotá. I came here to take a course at the Institute of Comparative Law. . . . I also work as an apprentice for Maître Puget, on Boulevard Raspail, very near here; he is a professor of international law."

"Are your parents rich?"

He answered rather apologetically:

"They are by Bogotá standards."

"Are you an only child?"

"I've got a younger brother, who is at Berkeley."

"Am I right in thinking your parents are Catholics, like most Colombians?"

"My mother is fairly devout."

"Are you going to take Madame Nahour to Bogotá?"

"I intend to."

"Don't you expect some trouble with your family if you marry a divorcee?"

"I'm over twenty-one."

"May I use your telephone?"

Maigret called the Hotel du Louvre.

"Lucas? . . . You can leave them alone. . . . But stay in the hotel. I'll have you relieved at the end of the afternoon."

Alvaredo smiled bitterly.

"You left one of your men in Lina's room to keep her from telephoning me, didn't you?"

"I'm sorry I have to take these precautions."

"I suppose your detective will watch me, too."

"I'm afraid so."

"Can I go and see her?"

"I don't see why not."

"Did the journey tire her?"

"Not enough for her to lose her presence of mind."

"She's a child."

"A very clever child."

"Won't you have a drink?"

"I'd rather not."

"Which means you still suspect me?"

"In my profession we suspect everybody."

On the sidewalk he sighed, drew a deep breath:

"There we are!"

"Do you think he lied, chief?"

Without answering, Maigret went on:

"You can get into your car. That red car will soon be racing toward Rue de Rivoli. Have a good afternoon . . . Keep in touch with the Quai so that you can be relieved."

"How about you?"

"I'm going back to Avenue du Parc-Montsouris. Tomorrow we'll have to get a few more men so that the interrogations can be made officially."

His hands in his pockets, he walked to the taxi stand at the corner of Boulevard Saint-Michel, cursing at the knitted scarf, which was bundled around his neck and tickled him.

From outside, the Nahours' house looked empty. The Superintendent told the driver to wait, crossed the little garden, where the snow creaked under his shoes, and pressed the bell.

A sleepy Torrence opened the door yawning.

"Anything new?"

"The father has arrived. He's in the study with his son."

"What's he like?"

"About seventy-five, with very thick white hair, a lined and energetic face."

The study door opened, and Pierre Nahour, recognizing Maigret, said:

"Do you need me, Superintendent?"

"I wanted to see Oueni."

"He's upstairs."

"Has your father met him?"

"Not yet. He'll undoubtedly have some questions to ask him later."

Maigret hung up his coat, his scarf, and his hat on the coatrack and went up the stairs. The hall was dark. He went to Fouad's room, knocked, and received an answer in Arabic.

When he opened the door he found Oueni sitting in an armchair. He was not reading. He wasn't doing anything. The face looking at Maigret was expressionless.

"You can come in. . . . What did they tell you?"

❧ 6 ❧

IT WAS THE MOST SIMPLE AND UNSOPHISTICATED ROOM IN
the house. The painter who had rented the house furnished to the Nahours must have had a young son,
because Oueni's room looked as though it had belonged
to a student. The secretary did not seem to have changed
anything, and there were no private possessions of his
to be seen.

Sitting in his leather armchair, his legs outstretched,
looking completely relaxed, the man was dressed as
punctiliously as the day before, in a well-cut dark suit.
He was closely shaven. His shirt was very white and his
nails manicured.

Appearing not to notice his insolent attitude, Maigret
stood in front of him and looked him straight in the
eye, as though he were sizing him up, and both men
looked like children trying not to blink.

"You're not very co-operative, Monsieur Oueni."

There was no sign of anxiety on the secretary's face.
His smile full of self-assurance and irony, he looked
almost as though he enjoyed flouting Maigret.

123

"Lina . . ."

Maigret emphasized this familiarity.

"I beg your pardon?"

"Madame Nahour, if you'd rather, doesn't quite agree about the way you spent your time on Friday evening. She claims that when she went into the study at about midnight you were there with Monsier Nahour. She says that you were standing next to him while he was sitting at his desk."

Maigret awaited an answer, which did not come. Fouad went on smiling.

"It's her word against mine, isn't it?" he said finally.

All through this conversation he spoke with the same calculated slowness, detaching every syllable.

"Do you deny it?"

"I answered your questions yesterday."

"That doesn't mean you told me the truth."

His fingers curled up on the arm of the chair as though he thought he had been insulted. Nevertheless, he controlled himself and said nothing.

The Superintendent walked to the window and stood for a while in front of it; then, his hands behind his back, his pipe in his mouth, he paced the room.

"You claim to have left the Bar des Tilleuls soon after one in the morning, and the owner has confirmed this. . . . On the other hand, he does not know when you arrived. . . . So far there is nothing to prove that you didn't just come in and out in order to establish an alibi."

"Have you questioned all the members of the club who were in the two gaming rooms that night?"

"You know perfectly well that we haven't had a

chance to do that yet and that the club and the bar are shut on Sunday."

"You have all the time you like. So have I."

Had he adopted this attitude just to infuriate Maigret? He had the coldness and nerve of a chess player, and it was going to be difficult to catch him out.

Stopping in front of him again the Superintendent asked mildly:

"Have you ever been married, Monsieur Oueni?"

And Oueni replied with a sentence that may have been a proverb in his country:

"He who is not satisfied with the pleasures a woman can give him in one night is putting a rope around his neck."

"That is what happened to Monsieur Nahour, I suppose?"

"His private life is none of my business."

"Have you ever had mistresses?"

"I'm not homosexual, if that's what you want to know."

This time his disdain was still more evident.

"I assume that means that you sometimes have affairs with women?"

"If French law is that curious, I can provide names and addresses."

"It wasn't a woman whom you went to see on Friday night?"

"No. I've already told you."

Maigret turned toward the window again and gazed vaguely at Avenue du Parc-Montsouris, covered with snow, where, despite the cold, there were occasional Sunday walkers.

"Have you got a gun, Monsieur Oueni?"

Fouad got up slowly, leaving his armchair almost reluctantly, opened a drawer in the chest, and pulled out a long pistol. It was not an object that could be carried in one's pocket but a training gun with a barrel at least twenty centimeters long and a caliber that did not correspond to the bullet found in Nahour's skull.

"Are you satisfied?"

"No."

"Have you asked Monsieur Alvaredo the same question?"

It was Maigret's turn not to answer. This interrogation went very slowly, like a game of chess, each man planning his attacks and retreats with care.

The Superintendent's face was serious. He took long puffs at his pipe, and the tobacco sizzled. They were surrounded by silence; they did not hear a sound from the quilted atmosphere outside.

"You know that Madame Nahour had been trying to get a divorce for almost two years?"

"I told you these questions are none of my business."

"In view of the intimacy of your relations with Monsieur Nahour it seems likely that he might have mentioned it to you."

"That's what you say."

"I'm not saying anything. I'm asking the questions and you're the one who isn't answering."

"I answer the questions that concern me."

"Did you also know that Madame Nahour had been planning for over a week to leave for Amsterdam and that this would mean final separation from her husband?"

"Ditto."

126

"Do you still claim not to have been in the room when this incident took place?"

Fouad shrugged his shoulders, considering the question superfluous.

"You have known Nahour for about twenty years. You hardly left his side in that time. He became a professional gambler, what one might call a scientific gambler, and you helped him in his calculations."

Oueni, who did not seem to be listening, had returned to his armchair. Grabbing a chair by its back, Maigret sat astride it less than a yard away from him.

"You arrived in Paris with hardly any money, didn't you? How much did Nahour pay you?"

"I was never paid a salary."

"Nevertheless, you needed money."

"When I did he gave it to me."

"Have you got a bank account?"

"No."

"How much did he give you at a time?"

"Whatever I asked for."

"Large amounts? Did you save?"

"I've never had anything but my clothes."

"Were you as able a gambler as he, Monsieur Oueni?"

"It's not for me to say."

"Did he ever suggest you should replace him at a roulette or baccarat table?"

"Occasionally."

"Did you win?"

"I lost and I won."

"Have you kept your winnings?"

"No."

"Was there ever any question of an association between you? For example, he could have given you a percentage of the sums he won."

He simply shook his head.

"So you were neither his associate nor his equal, since you were entirely dependent on him. Which means that in spite of everything you had a master-servant relationship. When he got married, weren't you afraid that your relationship might become less close?"

"No."

"Didn't Nahour love his wife?"

"You should have asked him."

"It's a bit late now. How long have you known that Madame Nahour had a lover?"

"Should I have known?"

If he thought he was making Maigret angry, he was wrong, because the Superintendent had rarely been in such control of himself.

"You can't not have known that the relationship between husband and wife, which had never been very intimate, had deteriorated over the last two years. You also knew how insistently Madame Nahour was demanding a divorce. Did you follow her, and who told your master about her affair with Alvaredo?"

A more disdainful smile than before.

"He saw them himself as they were coming out of a restaurant in the Palais-Royal. They didn't hide."

"Was Nahour in a rage?"

"I have never seen him in a rage."

"And yet, although he no longer had a sexual relationship with his wife and he knew that she loved someone else, he obliged her to live under the same roof. Wasn't that a form of revenge?"

"Maybe."

"And wasn't it after this discovery that he separated her from her children by sending them to the Riviera?"

"Unlike you, I don't read people's minds, whether they are dead or alive."

"I am sure that Madame Nahour was not lying when she said you were with her husband on Friday evening, Monsieur Oueni. I am even inclined to think that you knew about her journey and that you knew the date."

"I can't stop you."

"Her husband hated her. . . ."

"Didn't she hate him?"

"Let's say they hated each other. She had decided to be free, at all costs."

"At all costs. Exactly."

"Are you accusing Madame Nahour of killing her husband?"

"No."

"Are you accusing yourself?"

"No."

"Well?"

With calculated slowness, Oueni said:

"One person is interested in this business."

"Alvaredo?"

"Where was he?"

"In his car, by the door."

It was Fouad's turn to lead the interrogation, to ask the questions.

"Do you believe that?"

"Until I have proof of the contrary."

"He was very much in love, wasn't he?"

Maigret let him talk, curious to see what he was driving at.

"Probably."

"Very passionate. Didn't you say he'd been Madame Nahour's lover for two years? His parents wouldn't be very pleased to see him arrive with a divorcee and two children. The fact that he takes that risk suggests a great love, doesn't it?"

His eyes suddenly turned cruel, his mouth sarcastic.

"He knew how decisive the evening would be," he went on, still sitting motionless in the armchair. "Don't you agree?"

"Yes."

"Tell me, Monsieur Maigret, in his position and in his state of mind on Friday evening, would you have let your mistress face an obstinate husband alone? Do you really think he waited almost an hour outside without worrying for a moment about what was going on in the house?"

"Did you see him?"

"Don't set me such unsubtle traps. I didn't see anything, since I wasn't here. I'm simply showing you that that man's presence in the study is more plausible than mine."

Maigret got up, suddenly relaxed, as if he had finally got where he wanted.

"There were at least two people in the room," he said more lightly. "Nahour and his wife. That would imply that Madame Nahour was armed with a large revolver, which one can hardly hide in a handbag. Nahour would also have to fire first, and she would have had to kill him afterward."

"Not necessarily. She might have fired first, while her husband held the gun in his hand to defend himself, and it's quite possible that he automatically pressed the trigger as he fell, which would account for the inaccuracy."

"It doesn't much matter who fired first at the moment. Let us assume you were there. Madame Nahour took a gun out of her bag, and you fired in her direction to defend your employer, because you were near the drawer with the 6.35."

"That would suggest that she did not fire at me, because I was armed and could have shot back, but at her husband?"

"Let us assume that you hated the man you call Monsieur Felix. . . ."

"Why?"

"For years you've been a sort of poor relation, without really being a relation. You have no special function, but you look after everything, including the boiled eggs in the morning. You're not paid. You're given small sums—pocket money, in fact—when you need it.

"I don't know if the fact that you're of the same race matters or not. But in all events, your position was rather humiliating, and nothing stimulates hatred as much as humiliation.

"You have the chance to take revenge. Nahour shoots at his wife just when she goes to the door, never to come back. You shoot in your turn, not at her, but at him, knowing that she or her lover will be accused, after which you just need an alibi at the Club Saint-Michel.

"We have one way, Monsieur Fouad, of finding out

131

whether that is what happened, within an hour. I shall ring Moers, one of the best technicians at the Records Office. If he isn't at the Quai, he'll be at home. He will bring the equipment necessary for the test we performed on Monsieur Nahour, and we will know whether you used a firearm."

Oueni did not flinch. On the contrary, his smile became more ironical than ever.

As Maigret went toward the telephone, he stopped him:

"There's no point."

"Do you admit it?"

"You know as well as I do, Monsieur Maigret, that the test can reveal crusts of powder on the skin up to five days after a shot has been fired."

"You are remarkably knowledgeable."

"On Thursday I went to a shooting gallery, as I frequently do, in the basement of a gunsmith named Boutelleau and Sons, on Rue de Rennes."

"With your pistol?"

"No. I have another one, exactly like this one, which I leave there, like most of the customers. So it's quite likely that you'll find crusts of powder on my right hand."

"Why do you practice shooting?"

Maigret was annoyed.

"Because I belong to a tribe which goes armed at all times of the year and which claims to have produced the best shots in the world. Boys use guns after the age of ten."

Maigret slowly raised his head.

"And what if we don't find any traces of powder on Alvaredo's hand or on Madame Nahour's?"

"Alvaredo came from outdoors, where it was well below freezing. One can assume he was wearing gloves, and probably even fairly thick gloves. Didn't you check that?"

He was trying to be insulting.

"I'm sorry to have to do your job for you. Madame Nahour was getting ready to leave. I suppose she was wearing a coat and she probably put on her gloves."

"Is that your defense?"

"I didn't think I needed a defense until the Examining Magistrate accuses me."

"Please be at Quai des Orfèvres tomorrow at ten o'clock, where you will be interrogated officially. The magistrate you mention may well want to see you later."

"And until then?"

"You are not to leave the house, and one of my detectives will continue to watch you."

"I'm very patient, Monsieur Maigret."

"So am I, Monsieur Oueni."

Nevertheless, Maigret's cheeks were flushed when he left the room, although it may have been because of the heat. In the hall he gave a friendly nod to Torrence, who was sitting on a straight chair and reading a magazine, and knocked on the study door.

"Come in, Monsieur Maigret."

The two men stood up. The elder of the two, who was smoking a cigar, came toward the Superintendent and held out a dry and vigorous hand.

"I would rather have met you in different circumstances, Monsieur Maigret."

"Let me tell you how sorry I am. I didn't want to leave the house before saying that we are doing all we

133

can, the Police Judiciaire, and the Public Prosecutor, to find out who murdered your son."

"Have you got any clues?"

"I wouldn't go as far as to say that, but all the characters involved in this case are beginning to reveal their parts."

"Do you believe Felix shot at that woman?"

"That seems certain, either because he pressed the trigger involuntarily, or because he fired as a reflex after having been hit himself."

The father and son looked at each other in surprise.

"Do you think that that woman, who made him suffer so much, finally . . . "

"I'm not yet in a position to accuse anybody. Good night, gentlemen."

"Shall I stay here?" asked Torrence a little later in the hall.

"Fouad is not to go out. I'd rather have you on the next floor and know about any phone calls he makes. I don't yet know who'll be relieving you."

The taxi driver muttered:

"I thought you were staying only a few minutes!"

"The Hotel du Louvre."

"I won't wait for you there. I started work at eleven and I haven't had time for lunch yet."

Night was falling. The driver must have run the engine occasionally, because inside the taxi the air was hot.

Maigret, huddled in the back seat, gazed vaguely at the black and chilly figures sliding past the buildings, and he wasn't really sure how satisfied with himself he was.

Lucas was dozing, his hands on his stomach, in one of the monumental armchairs in the hall. When he saw, through his drooping lids, the Superintendent coming toward him, he jumped up and asked, rubbing his eyes:

"Everything all right, chief?"

"Yes . . . No . . . Has Alvaredo arrived?"

"Not yet . . . None of the ladies have gone out. . . . One of them, the friend, went downstairs and bought some newspapers and magazines at the end of the hall. . . ."

Maigret hesitated, then muttered:

"Are you thirsty?"

"I had a glass of beer a quarter of an hour ago. . . ."

Maigret went to the bar by himself, left his coat, hat, and scarf in the checkroom, and leaned one buttock against a tall stool. There was hardly anybody there except for the barman's assistant, who was listening to a soccer match on the radio.

"Whisky," he ordered.

He needed one before the task he had decided to undertake. Where had he read the maxim "Always attack at the point of least resistance"?

He had been thinking about it on the way, in the taxi. Four people knew the truth, or part of the truth, about the Nahour case. He had questioned all four of them, some of them twice. They had all lied, on at least one point, if not on several.

Who, of the four, would offer least resistance?

At one moment he had thought of Nelly Velthuis, whose ingenuousness could not have been entirely false, but precisely because she didn't realize the importance of her lies, she might have told him anything.

135

Alvaredo was really quite nice. He was a passionate man. His love for Lina seemed sincere, and fervent, so that he would not say a word that could injure the young woman.

Maigret had just left Oueni, who was clever enough to foresee and to avoid every trap.

There remained Lina, about whom he hesitated to come to a conclusion. At first sight she was a child struggling among grownups, without knowing which way to turn.

Starting as a little switchboard operator in Amsterdam, she had been attracted by the more glamorous career of a fashion model before thoughtlessly entering a beauty contest.

Then the miracle happened, and from one day to the next the girl found herself in a completely strange world.

A rich man, playing for high stakes every night and to whom the staff of the casino bowed low, sent her flowers and invited her to dinner in the best restaurants without asking for anything in exchange.

He took her to Biarritz, as discreetly as ever, and on the night when he summoned up enough courage to enter her room, he immediately proposed marriage to her.

How could she have understood the psychology of someone like Nahour? Or, still less, of Fouad Oueni, who followed the couple everywhere for no apparent reason?

When she wanted to have a Dutch maid, it was as though she had called for help, and she had chosen—from a photograph?—the most ingenuous and gayest candidate.

She had had expensive dresses, jewels, and furs, but in Deauville, Cannes, and Evian, wherever she was taken without being asked her opinion, she was alone, and she occasionally went to Amsterdam to talk openly to Anna Keegel as she had done when the two girls shared the apartment on Lomanstraat.

She had had a child. Was she prepared for motherhood? Was it for fear that the responsibility might be too great for her that Nahour had called in a nurse?

Had she had lovers and affairs since then?

The years went by, and her features remained as young, her skin as clear and smooth as ever. But her mind? Had she learned anything?

Another child, a son, finally satisfied the husband who had slept with her for only a fairly brief period.

She met Alvaredo. Her life suddenly took on new color. . . .

Maigret was starting to feel sorry for her, and then told himself:

Nevertheless, it's the little girl with innocent eyes who started this whole business. . . .

And who had been behaving remarkably coolly ever since Friday evening.

He almost ordered another whisky, decided against it, and took the elevator to the fourth floor a few seconds later. Nelly opened the door of the sitting room.

"Is Madame Nahour asleep?"

"No. She's having tea."

"Will you tell her I want to see her?"

He found her sitting up in bed, a white silk bed jacket over her shoulders, reading an English or American magazine. The tea and the slices of cake were on the bed table, and Anna Keegel, who must have been lying on the second bed when the Superintendent arrived, ran her hand over her hair and assumed an aggressive posture.

"I'd like to talk to you alone, Madame Nahour."

"Can't Anna stay? I've never hidden anything from her and . . . "

"Let's say that I mind her being here."

It was almost true. When the door was shut, Maigret brought a chair up between the two beds and sat on it clumsily.

"Have you seen Vicente? Is he very worried about me?"

"I told him you were all right, and you did, too, on the telephone. I suppose you're expecting him?"

"In half an hour. I told him to come at half past five because I thought I'd sleep longer. What did you think of him?"

"He seems very much in love. It's about him that I'd like to ask you my first question, Madame Nahour. I understand that you're doing all you can to keep him out of this business and to keep his name out of it, since that would make his and your future relationship with his parents more difficult.

"As for me, I shall avoid getting him any publicity as far as I can.

"But one detail worries me. You told me he stayed in his car on Friday evening all the time you were in the house—that is to say, about an hour.

"He knew about your decision. He realized that your husband would not hear of a divorce. He could therefore have expected a stormy and dramatic meeting.

Why, then, did he leave you alone instead of sharing the responsibility?"

As he spoke she bit her lower lip.

"That's the truth," she said simply.

"Oueni has a different opinion."

"What did he tell you?"

"That Alvaredo came into the study with you, and he added a further detail: that your companion was wearing heavy winter gloves. Oueni also says that when your husband fired, it was Alvaredo who pulled a pistol out of his pocket and fired in his turn."

"Oueni's lying."

"I am inclined to believe that you first had a violent discussion with your husband while Alvaredo stood discreetly near the door. When Nahour realized that your decision was final, he threatened you, after pulling the 6.35 out of the drawer. Thinking he was going to shoot, your friend fired first, to protect you, and Nahour pressed the trigger as he fell."

"That's not what happened."

"Correct me."

"I've already told you. To begin with, if Vicente stayed in the car it's because I wanted him to. I even told him I wouldn't come with him if he came into the house."

"Was your husband sitting at his desk?"

"Yes."

"And Oueni?"

"Stood on his right."

"So he was in front of the drawer with the gun."

"I think so. . . . "

"You think so or are you sure?"

"I'm sure."

139

"Did Oueni look as though he were going to leave the room?"

"He moved, but he didn't leave."

"In which direction did he move?"

"Toward the middle of the room."

"Before you spoke or after you had started speaking?"

"After."

"You told me you didn't like him. Why didn't you ask your husband to send him out?"

"Felix would have refused. Besides, by that time I didn't care any more."

"What was the first thing you said?"

"I said:

" ' There you are! I've made up my mind and that's final. I'm leaving. . . . ' "

"Were you speaking French?"

"English. I learned English when I was very young, but I only learned French much later."

"What did your husband say?"

" ' With your lover? Is he waiting in the car?' "

"What was Nahour like just then?"

"Very pale, with set features. He got up slowly, and I think it was then that he opened the drawer, but I didn't know what he was going to do. I added that I wasn't angry with him, that I thanked him for all he'd done for me, that it was up to him to decide about the children, and that my lawyer would get in touch with him. . . . "

"Where was Oueni?"

"I didn't pay any attention to him. Not far from me, I suppose. He never makes much noise."

"Was that when your husband fired?"

"No. Not yet. He repeated what he had often told me, that he would never accept a divorce. I told him he'd have to. Only then did I realize he was holding a gun. . . . "

"And then?"

Maigret was leaning slightly toward her, as though to stop her escaping again.

"The two . . . "

She corrected herself:

"The shot was fired."

"No. The two shots, as you were about to say. I'm sure Alvaredo was in the study but he didn't fire."

"Do you think I did?"

"Not you either. Oueni pulled the gun out of his pocket before or after your husband fired. . . . "

"As long as I was in the house there was only one shot. Nelly will confirm it."

"Nelly lies almost as much as you do, my dear."

This time it was a menacing Maigret who got up. He had stopped playing. After putting his chair back in the corner, he strode around the room, and Lina no longer recognized the man who had seemed almost paternal shortly before.

"At one point, and the sooner the better, you will have to stop lying. Otherwise I'll call the Examining Magistrate at once and ask for a warrant for your arrest."

"Why should Oueni have shot at my husband?"

"Because he loved you."

"Him? Fouad, love someone?"

"Don't pretend to be innocent, Lina. How long after

your first meeting with Nahour did Oueni become your lover?"

"Did he tell you?"

"It doesn't matter. Answer me . . . "

"Several months after my marriage. . . . I didn't expect it. . . . I'd never seen him with a woman. . . . He seemed to despise them. . . ."

"Did you decide to excite him?"

"Is that what you think of me?"

"I'm sorry. Besides, it doesn't matter who started it. Until then he had almost belonged to Nahour. But now he partly escaped him because of you. By becoming your lover he could pay back every humiliation, past and future."

She had suddenly become almost ugly. Her features faded away, and she cried without trying to dry her tears.

"In the hotels and villas where you lived, and you and your husband had separate rooms, it was easy for Oueni to come and see you at night. So on Avenue du Parc-Montsouris . . . "

"Nothing ever happened there. . . ."

She was really upset and she looked at him with imploring eyes.

"I swear it! When it became serious with Alvaredo . . ."

"What do you mean?"

"When I realized that he really loved me and that I loved him, I stopped seeing Fouad."

"Who agreed to this little break?"

"He tried in every way, once even by force, to resume our affair. . . ."

"How long ago?"

"About a year and a half ago."

"Did you know he still loved you?"

"Yes."

"Weren't you turning the knife in the wound by talking to your husband that evening when he was there?"

"I didn't think of that."

"If he moved near you at the beginning of the conversation, wasn't he trying to protect you?"

"I didn't think about that. At the end I didn't even know where he was standing."

"Were the two shots almost simultaneous?"

She didn't answer. She was obviously exhausted and wasn't acting anymore. Her shoulders had sunk into the pillows and her body was curled up under the sheet.

"Why didn't you tell the truth when I first questioned you?"

"About what?"

"About the shot fired by Fouad."

She answered in a whisper:

"Because I didn't want Vicente to know . . ."

"To know what?"

"About Fouad and me. I was ashamed. I'd had an affair, a long time ago in Cannes, and I told him. But not about Fouad! If I accuse him, he'll say everything at the trial and our marriage will never be possible. . . ."

"Wasn't Alvaredo surprised to see Oueni kill your husband?"

They looked straight at each other for several seconds. Maigret's eyes gradually lost their hardness, while

Lina's blue eyes showed more and more fatigue and resignation.

"He dragged me out, and in the car I told him Fouad had always hated my husband. . . ."

Her lower lip was slightly swollen. She added, under her breath:

"Why were you so unkind to me, Monsieur Maigret?"

❧ 7 ❧

AT ELEVEN O'CLOCK ON MONDAY MORNING MAIGRET LEFT one of the offices on Quai des Orfèvres where he had just officially interrogated his fourth witness.

He had started with Alvaredo, whom he had asked about twenty questions, and Lapointe had taken down the questions and the answers in shorthand. Of all these, there had been one of major importance, and the young Colombian had taken his time.

"Think well, Monsieur Alvaredo. It's probably the last time that I'll interrogate you, because from now on the case will be in the hands of the Examining Magistrate. Were you in the car or in the house?"

"In the house. Lina opened the door before going into the study."

"Was Nahour still alive?"

"Yes."

"Was anyone else in the room?"

"Fouad Oueni."

"Where were you standing?"

"By the door."

"Did Nahour try to make you leave?"

"He pretended not to see me."

"Where was Fouad Oueni when the shots were fired?"

"About a yard away from Lina, in the middle of the room."

"That is to say, at a certain distance from Nahour?"

"Just over three yards."

"Who fired first?"

"I think Oueni did, but I'm not sure because the two shots were almost simultaneous."

Then, while the young Colombian had awaited permission to leave, it had been Anna Keegel's turn in the next-door office, and her interrogation had been fairly brief.

In the third office, he had been quite lenient with Nelly Velthuis, who was very surprised.

"How many shots did you hear?"

"I don't know."

"Could there have been two shots, almost simultaneously?"

"I think so."

As for Lina, he had made her repeat most of what she had said the day before, but did not mention her affair with Fouad.

It had stopped snowing. The weather was getting damper and the snow was turning to slush. There were the usual drafts in the vast hallway of the Police Judiciaire, but the offices were overheated.

There was a certain excitement in the whole building, because all the detectives, even those who were not on the Crime Squad, had realized that an important operation was going on.

Newspapermen, with the inevitable Maquille among them, were sitting on the benches and they assaulted the Superintendent every time he went into an office.

"In a minute boys, I'm not ready. . . ."

God knows how—probably by questioning the staff at Orly—a morning paper had found out about Lina's short trip to Amsterdam in the company of a mysterious character called Monsieur X. That meant that the case was going to take a sensational turn, which Maigret did not like.

He still had to see Oueni.

When the Superintendent had gone home on Sunday evening at about seven, after passing by the Quai, Madame Maigret could see at a glance how he felt.

"Tired?"

"It's not so much tiredness."

"Disheartened?"

"It's a foul job!" he had muttered, as he did every two or three years in cases like this. "I haven't got the right to close my eyes and ears, and if I don't, I run the risk of ruining the existence of people who don't deserve it."

She had taken care not to ask him any questions, and after dinner they had watched television in silence.

At the end of the hallway, he drew a deep breath and sighed:

"Come on, Lapointe."

He still had hope. He opened the door of the office in which Oueni was sitting and found him, as usual, deep in the only armchair in the room, his legs stretched out in front of him.

As on the day before, the secretary did not get up,

did not even greet the two men, whom he looked at in turn with cruel irony.

Maigret remembered Voltaire's "hideous smile" from his school days, and because he had stood before the bust of the great man, Maigret had never approved of this expression. Since then he had seen many arrogant, aggressive, and perfidious smiles, but this was the first time that the word "hideous" came to mind.

He sat on a chair at a white wooden table covered with brown paper on which stood a typewriter. Lapointe sat at the narrow end of the table and put his pad in front of him.

"Your name and given name."

"Oueni, Fouad, born in Takla, Lebanon."

"Age."

"Fifty-one."

Pulling a foreign resident's card from his pocket he held it out, but did not leave his armchair, so that Lapointe had to get up.

"The French police confirm it," he said ironically.

"Profession?"

"Legal adviser."

As he said these two words his voice became still more bantering.

"It's your police that say it. Read it . . ."

"Were you at any moment on Friday, January 14, between eleven in the evening and one in the morning, in the study of your employer, Monsieur Felix Nahour, on Avenue du Parc-Montsouris?"

"No. Please note that Monsieur Nahour was not my employer, since I wasn't getting a salary."

"In what capacity did you follow him to his various

houses and in particular to Avenue du Parc-Mont-souris?"

"As a friend."

"You weren't his secretary?"

"I helped him when he needed my advice."

"Where were you on Friday evening after eleven?"

"At the Saint-Michel Club, to which I belong."

"Can you mention the names of a few people who saw you there?"

"I don't know who saw me."

"How many people would you say were in the two fairly small rooms of the club?"

"Between twenty and thirty, depending on the time."

"You didn't talk to anybody?"

"No. I wasn't there to talk but to note the winning numbers at roulette."

"Where were you standing?"

"Behind the players. I was sitting in a corner by the door."

"What time did you arrive at Boulevard Saint-Michel?"

"About half past ten."

"What time did you leave the club?"

"About one in the morning."

"So you claim that you were surrounded by over thirty people for two and a half hours without anybody noticing you?"

"I didn't say anything like that."

"But you can't mention a single name."

"I had no dealings with the other gamblers, who are mainly students."

"On your way out you went through the bar on the ground floor? Did you talk to anyone?"

"To the owner."

"What did you say to him?"

"That four had come up over eight times in under an hour."

"How did you get back to Avenue du Parc-Montsouris?"

"By car."

"Monsieur Nahour's Bentley?"

"Yes. I usually drove it, and it was at my disposal."

"Three witnesses claim that you were standing in Monsieur Nahour's study, on his right, at about midnight."

"They all have a reason to lie."

"What did you do when you came back?"

"I went up to my room and went to bed."

"Without opening the door of the study?"

"Yes."

"You've been living off Felix Nahour for twenty years, Oueni, and he's been treating you like a poor relation. You acted not only as secretary, but also as valet and chauffeur. Weren't you humiliated by this?"

"I was grateful for the confidence he showed in me, and it was of my own free will that I did him small favors."

He continued to look at Maigret defiantly, almost jubilantly. The words that he said could be taken down and used as evidence against him, so he chose them with care. But it was impossible to reproduce on paper his expressions, which were a constant defiance.

"Didn't you feel frustrated when Monsieur Nahour got married after having lived alone with you for nearly fifteen years?"

"Our relationship was not in any way governed by passion, if that's what you're implying, and I had no reason for being jealous."

"Was your employer happily married?"

"He didn't confide in me about his married life."

"Do you think Madame Nahour was satisfied with the life she was leading with her husband, particularly during the last two years?"

"I never thought about that."

This time Maigret's face grew heavier, as though it contained a message, and Oueni understood it. Nevertheless, by emphasizing a sort of silent defiance, he sustained his cynical attitude, which contrasted with the objectivity of his replies.

"What was your relationship with Madame Nahour?"

"I had nothing whatsoever to do with her."

Now that the interrogation was official, intended to play a part of capital importance in the future, every word was loaded with dynamite.

"Didn't you try to seduce her?"

"It never occurred to me."

"Did you ever happen to be alone in a room with her?"

"If you mean a bedroom, the answer is no."

"Think carefully."

"No again."

"A 7.65-caliber gun has been found in your room. Do you possess another pistol, and if so, where is it now?"

"At a gunsmith's on Rue de Rennes, where I often used to go and practice."

"When did you last go there?"

151

"On Thursday."

"Thursday the 13th—that is to say, the day before the murder. Did you then know that Madame Nahour intended to leave her husband the next day?"

"She didn't confide in me."

"Her maid knew."

"Nelly and I were not on very good terms."

"Because you tried to go to bed with her and she rejected you?"

"It was more the other way around."

"So this shooting session on Thursday was at a convenient time to explain why you probably have crusts of powder on your fingers. At least two people were present on Friday evening, shortly before or after midnight, in Monsieur Nahour's study. Both of them swear under oath that you were there, too."

"Who are these two people?"

"First, Madame Nahour."

"And what was she doing there?"

"She had come to tell her husband that she was leaving that night and to ask for a divorce."

"Did you tell you that her husband was prepared to give her a divorce? Was it the first time that she had mentioned it to him? Didn't she know that he would do everything in his power to oppose it?"

"Including shooting at her?"

"Have you proved that he fired intentionally? Finally, have you frequently found that people aim at the throat at two or three yards' range? Did Madame Nahour also tell you why she was suddenly so impatient about the divorce?"

"To marry Vicente Alvaredo, who was in the room with her when the shot was fired."

"One or more shots?"

"There were two shots, almost simultaneously, and it seems to have been the first that hit Nahour in the throat."

"Which means that the second shot was fired by a dead man?"

"Death was not necessarily instantaneous. Nahour could have pressed the trigger without realizing it, while he was bleeding profusely and staggering to the ground."

"Who would have fired the first shot?"

"You."

"Why?"

"Maybe to protect Lina Nahour, maybe out of hatred for your employer."

"Why not Alvaredo?"

"He apparently has never used a gun in his life and did not possess one. The investigation will or will not confirm this point."

"Didn't they run away?"

"They went to Amsterdam, as they had planned to do for a week, and they returned to Paris as soon as the Dutch police advised them to."

"On your behalf? After you had promised that they wouldn't get into trouble? Was Monsieur Alvaredo wearing gloves?"

"He was."

"Weren't they thick leather gloves, which haven't been found?"

"They were found last night at Orly, and the laboratory found no trace of powder on them."

"Wasn't Madame Nahour, who was just about to leave, also wearing gloves?"

"The same test had no result."

"Are you sure they are the same gloves?"

"The maid has confirmed it."

"At the beginning you mentioned three witnesses. I suppose the third is Nelly Velthuis?"

"She was leaning over the banister on the second floor waiting for the end of the conversation and she heard two shots."

"Did she tell you that on Saturday?"

"That's none of your business."

"Can you tell me where she spent Sunday?"

"In the Hotel du Louvre with her mistress and a friend of hers."

"Didn't these three people receive any calls, apart from you? Because I suppose you went to interrogate them, just as you interrogated me on Avenue du Parc-Montsouris."

"Alvaredo went to see them at the end of the afternoon."

Then Oueni said dryly, reversing the roles:

"That's all. From now on I'll talk only in the presence of my lawyer."

"There is, however, one question that I have already asked you and that I want to repeat: What was your relationship with Madame Nahour?"

Oueni had an icy smile, and his eyes were darker and brighter than ever when he spat out:

"I had nothing to do with her."

"Thank you, Lapointe. Will you call two detectives?"

He had got up and gone around the table. He stood in front of Oueni, who was still in his chair. Looking him up and down, the Superintendent asked bitterly:

"Revenge?"

Fouad then looked around the room, to make sure they were alone and the door was shut, and said:

"Perhaps."

"Stand up."

He obeyed.

"Hold out your wrists."

He did so, without losing his smile.

"I arrest you on a warrant from Examining Magistrate Cayotte. . . ."

Then to the two inspectors who came in:

"Take this man to the police station."

❧ 8 ❧

IT HAD BECOME THE "NAHOUR CASE." FOR A WEEK IT WAS on the front pages of all the papers and had several columns in the sensationalizing weeklies. Newspapermen were permanently prowling around Avenue du Parc-Montsouris, picking up gossip, and Madame Bodin, the cleaning woman, had her hour of glory.

Maquille went to Amsterdam, then to Cannes, and returned with an interview with the nurse and a photograph of her and the children. He also questioned the casino managers and croupiers.

All this time the men from the Records Office were going through the Nahour's house with a fine-tooth comb, in the hope of finding some clue. They also went through the garden, and even searched the drains for the pistol that had killed Nahour.

The meeting with the lawyer had taken place on Monday afternoon, in the presence of Pierre Nahour, his father, and Lina.

Maigret was told about it on the telephone by Maître Leroy-Beaulieu. In his second will Felix Nahour did not leave his wife any more than the legal minimum. The rest went to the children, and he expressed the desire that they be entrusted to the care of his brother and that if this were impossible, they be appointed an alternative guardian.

"Didn't he leave Oueni anything?"

"I was amazed. I can now tell you that in his first will, which was canceled by this one, Nahour left a sum of five hundred thousand francs to his secretary, 'in return for his devotion and services.' Well, Oueni's name isn't even mentioned in the final will."

Had Nahour found out in the meantime about Fouad's affair with Lina?

Thirty-six patrons of the Saint-Michel Club, the manager, and the croupiers were questioned by the Examining Magistrate.

The newspapermen were waiting for them as they came out, and this provoked incidents after certain furious witnesses rushed at the photographers.

There were also some mistakes. A Cambodian student said he had seen Oueni sitting in the corner from eleven o'clock that evening. It took two days' patient investigation to discover that this student had never set foot in the club on Friday; he was mixing it up with the previous Wednesday.

Some neighbors who came home at half past eleven after having spent the evening at the movies swore that they had not seen a car parked in front of the bar.

The Magistrate, Cayotte, was a thorough and patient man. For three months he summoned Maigret to his office almost every day to ask him to make further investigations.

In the papers, politics took first place again, and the

Nahour case was relegated to the third and then to the fifth page, before it disappeared completely.

Lina, Alvaredo, and Nelly were not allowed to leave Paris without permission, and it was only after the investigation was over that they were permitted to hide in a little house near Dreux.

The Grand Jury confirmed Oueni's indictment but the calendars of the Assize Court were so full that the case was not tried until the following January, a year after Doctor Pardon had received the silent wounded woman and her lover in his office on Boulevard Voltaire.

Curiously enough the two men never alluded to the Nahour case during their monthly dinners.

One day a slightly flushed Maigret had to give his evidence in court. Until then nothing had been said about Lina's affair with the defendant.

The Superintendent replied as objectively and briefly as possible to the Judge's questions. As soon as he saw the Public Prosecutor get up he knew that the young woman's secret was in danger.

"May I question the witness, your Honor?"

"The Public Prosecutor may proceed."

"Can the witness tell the jury whether he has reason to believe that there was ever an intimate relationship between the defendant and Madame Nahour?"

The Superintendent was under oath and could not cheat.

"Yes."

"Has the defendant denied this formally?"

"Yes."

"Nevertheless, his attitude suggests that this is true?"

"Yes."

"Does the witness believe in this relationship?"

"Yes."

"Did this knowledge contribute to Oueni's arrest by throwing a new light on his motives?"

"Yes."

That was all. The spectators had listened in silence, but now there was uproar in the courtroom and the Judge had to use his gavel.

"If order is not restored, I shall clear the court. . . ."

Maigret had the chance to sit next to Cayotte, who had kept a place for him. But he preferred to leave.

When he was alone in the deserted hallways, in which his steps echoed, he slowly filled a pipe without realizing what he was doing.

A few minutes later he was at the bar in the Palais de Justice and ordered a beer in a surly voice.

He didn't have the courage to go home. He drank another beer, almost in one draught, and then walked slowly toward Quai des Orfèvres.

It wasn't snowing this year. The air was mild. It was like early spring, and the sun was so bright that one expected the buds to burst into flower.

Back in his office he opened the door of the detectives' room.

"Lucas! . . . Janvier! . . . Lapointe! . . ."

It was as though all three were waiting for him.

"Take your coats and come with me. . . ."

They followed him without asking where they were going. A few minutes later they went up the worn steps of the Brasserie Dauphine.

"Well, Monsieur Maigret, how about the Nahour case?" said the owner.

He regretted his question, because the Superintendent looked at him and shrugged his shoulders. He quickly added:

"There's *andouillette* today, you know. . . ."

The couple could no longer go to Bogotá. And would the relationship between Lina and Alvaredo ever be the same after that morning's session?

The Nahour case was back in the headlines. For the evening papers it was the story of a ménage à quatre.

Without the new motive, on which the Public Prosecutor based his case, the jury might have acquitted Oueni.

The weapon had not been found. The charge was based only on the evidence of more or less interested parties.

The next evening Fouad Oueni was sentenced to ten years' imprisonment, while Lina and Alvaredo, who had been let out through a side door, got into the Alfa Romeo and drove off to an unknown destination.

Maigret never heard about them again.

"I've failed," he admitted to Pardon, with whom he dined on the following Tuesday.

"Maybe if I hadn't called you that night . . ."

"Events would nevertheless have taken their course, after a slight delay. . . ."

And Maigret added, reaching for his glass of Marc de Bourgogne:

"Oueni really won. . . ."